Alice Flanagan is a Sydney-based author and mother of two. Following university, her career path was far from that of a writer and included several years as a teacher, then a career as a computer programmer and business analyst.
Ecstasy is her second novel. Her first, Raindance, was published in 2006.

IN THE SAME SERIES

Ecstasy

A.C.FLANAGAN

Ransom

Peterborough City Council	
60000 0000 40474	
Askews & Holts	Jan-2012
GET ON	£5.99

Ecstasy
A.C.FLANAGAN

Series Editor: Peter Lancett

Published by Ransom Publishing Ltd.
Radley House, 8 St. Cross Road, Winchester, Hampshire, SO23 9HX, UK
www.ransom.co.uk

ISBN 978 184167 8818

First published in 2010
Copyright © 2010 Ransom Publishing Ltd.
Front cover photograph: David Maczkowiack

*Dedicated to all young minds
and the choice not to let
drugs fuck them up.*

CHAPTER 1

I am just 17 and my life is over. Head spinning, hands shaking, I need to throw up again. The lights are so bright I can only squint. I can hear people passing, but they're just blurs.

Sitting here, sweat carving lines through my make-up, I feel as if everyone is judging me. The seats either side of me are empty. People are standing, rather than sit next to me – the junkie. Funny, isn't it, that I'm drowning in a sea of people, but if I died in front of them, it'd be alone.

I came here with Mai-Ling but they took her away, through those clear plastic swing doors. She was totally out of it. I thought she had just partied too hard when she fell on the footpath and started throwing up. But then blood started trickling from her ears and nose and I panicked. I got her here as fast as I could but it was hard, no-one would help. I haven't seen her since and nobody's telling me what is happening.

You think I am self-pitying. You're thinking I'm another spoilt rich kid whose daddy gave her everything. Shit, they called the cops before they called my father!

The only time anyone comes near me is to question me again. They want to know everything but I can hardly think, let alone focus on what they are saying. I'm still too smashed to concentrate and they know it, but they keep hammering me. I don't care what they want to know, I just keep on back at them: "Is Mai-Ling OK? Is my friend alright?"

They act like they don't hear me.

On and on they go with the same fucking questions, "What did your friend take? What did she drink? When did she start losing consciousness?"

I keep saying to them, I've already told you everything – just leave me alone!

Fuck, I'm going to throw up again!

It's been half an hour since I spewed but my stomach won't settle. My father is still not here, even though I've called him like a million times. I have no-one and I'm scared.

"Carrie Jones?" a voice startles me from behind. As I turn I am face to face with two cops. I can hear the whole waiting room exhale. The cavalry has arrived! Someone to take the druggie away.

"Carrie?"

They want me to talk to them but the room is spinning and I can only hold my head in my hands and nod.

"I am Constable Adams and this is Constable Cummings; we need to ask you about what happened tonight."

Taking my hands from my face, the neon lights burn. I see a woman who could only be three or four years older than I am. The realisation is starting to hit me that I'm in a shit-load of trouble and things have gone way too far. If the police are here then something really terrible must have happened to Mai-Ling. Or am I still tripping and this is not real. But it feels real – too real.

I swallow hard to stop the tears, "Is Mai-Ling . . .?"

The Constable's face is blank as she glances at her partner. It is as if they are talking in some kind of silent code to each other.

"Is she alright?"

Still no answer.

"Is she?" I am screaming now, I need to know! "For Christ's sake, will someone tell me what is happening with Mai-Ling?"

My words have poured themselves into my tears and I can hardly catch my breath. "She was just pinging, right? You know, she's just high. She'll be okay now that she's spewed, right?"

The female cop sits down next to me and looks me straight in the eye. She's freaking me out. My heart is racing and sweat is pouring down my face. My hair is dripping wet and I can't stop shaking. She is still just staring at me like she's searching for a way to break the terrible news to me.

She puts her hand on my shoulder. "Mai-Ling is still unconscious. This is very serious. We don't know yet . . ."

I feel like I have been hit in the guts. "What do you mean it's serious? She hardly took anything!"

The other cop stands and holds out his hand. "Let's go and sit down somewhere quieter, Carrie."

"Let me see Mai-Ling. You can make the doctors let me see her, I know you can."

"The best way to help Mai-Ling at the moment is to tell us everything that happened tonight."

"I've told them everything. I don't know anything else."

"I know but we need to ask you some more things."

"What things?"

"Come on, let's find a quieter place."

This guy is making out like he wants to help me but I don't trust him. My father has told me a lot about how the police get people to say things which get you into trouble. He's got a shit-load of stories about how they pretend to be your friend but really they're just trying to get you to say something bad. I don't trust them.

"I need my father to be here. He's a lawyer. I can't speak to you until he's here."

They stiffen the minute I say "lawyer". They're going to start pressuring me now, I can tell.

The woman cop is smiling at me with this fake I-care-about-you smile. "Carrie, Mai-Ling's mother is on her way. Don't you think she deserves to know what happened?"

"I already told the doctors what she took."

"You told them she had a tablet at a party. What was it?"

"I already told them."

"You need to tell us."

"Fuck! It was an ecstasy tablet. Okay?"

"Who did she get it from?"

"From this guy at the party. He had lots. Everyone was taking them. If there was something wrong we'd all be sick, right?"

The male cop keeps looking straight at me and asks his next question. "What's the name of the person who gave Mai-Ling the tablet?"

"I need to see my father! Where the *fuck* is my father?"

"I don't know where your father is, but Carrie, we need to know now. You want to help Mai-Ling, don't you?"

"Of course I fucking want to help Mai-Ling. She's my best friend! What do you think I am?"

"Did you take one of the tablets as well?"

"No."

"You took something though."

"What does that matter?"

The female cop stares at me again like she's my mother. Stupid bitch, she thinks she's so cool in her uniform and that shiny badge.

"I took a half, okay. I told Mai-Ling to only take a half. She hadn't taken it before and I told her to just take a half. But she didn't listen!"

"Can you tell us what happened from the beginning? From when you got to the party?"

"I need my father here first."

The woman cop looks over at her partner. He is shaking his head. I hear him whispe something like, "Go steady on her, she's just a kid." The woman cop is glaring back and I can't make out what she's saying. The guy cop sits down next to me.

"Look, I know this is hard for you. Your friend is really sick and you're feeling pretty sick yourself. We're not trying to make things harder for you."

"I need to call my father."

As I fumble for my mobile phone it starts to ring. "Dad?"

It's not him but his girlfriend, Anne.

"I need to speak to my dad."

She is telling me that he is out at the moment but she will get him to call me the minute he gets back.

"ed him to come now . . ."

 eady hung up. She treats me Fuck! I'm in the hospital

for Christ's sake and his girlfriend is screening his calls! I want to cry but I need to scream.

The woman cop is looking at me like she actually understands. "Come on, let's go to the Ladies and you can wash your face."

The mention of water reminds me how thirsty I am. Now, I cannot think of anything else.

"I need water."

She brings me a plastic cup. I scull it and am desperate for more. She brings me one cup after another. It's like I'm a bloody camel.

I'm still drinking when a woman runs into the waiting room screaming Mai-Ling's name. She stops dead, looks at me and my whole stomach knots. It is Mai-Ling's mum and she looks like a train wreck, clothes thrown over pyjamas. Jesus, she is walking over to me, face screwed up. She has no idea.

"Carrie, Carrie, where's my Mai-Ling? What's happened to her?"

She is so unaware, she has no fucking clue.

"I don't know, Mrs Truong. She's in with the doctors I think."

She looks at the two cops and then back at me. "Carrie, what's going on?"

The policewoman saves me from answering. She moves Mai-Ling's mum away and starts talking to her. God, I feel like crap. She is crying and clutching at the policewoman guiding her over to one of the nurses. The other cop is still sitting with me. He is watching Mai-Ling's mother too and I know what he is thinking. How glad he is that it's not him having to tell her; how thankful he is that he is the one left here with me. He is like my father, unemotional when it comes to real life. He catches me looking at him and makes an oh-shit kind of face. I make the same and decide that my father can do what he does best, arrive in time to clean up the mess.

"My dad's not coming. What do you want me to tell you?"

———

We wait in a small office to the side of the waiting room. I see Mai-Ling's mum through the glass, sitting in the waiting room crying. Others are watching her but no-one goes to see if she's alright. I should be with her but instead I am here telling two strangers how her daughter came to be passed out in the emergency unit of the Royal Prince Alfred Hospital.

The policewoman leans towards me. "We need to know exactly what happened tonight. From the beginning."

"There isn't much to tell. It was just some stupid party with a bunch of stupid people getting drunk and off their faces."

"Can you tell me where this party was? The address?"

"Somewhere in Newtown, near the train station."

The other cop chimes in. "Carrie we need you to be more exact."

"That's all I know. We went there with these guys we met in the city."

The policewoman asks, "Did you know these people?"

"No, not really, we met them at a nightclub earlier on. They said they were going to this party and said we could come."

"How old are you, Carrie?"

"Seventeen."

"And Mai-Ling?"

"Seventeen."

I can tell she is thinking that I'm trash. I have a private education, go to one of the best private schools in Sydney, but I'm still trash. None the less she is keeping up her I-really-care-about-you tone.

"Okay, what happened when you got to the party?"

"We had a couple of drinks and kind of hung around a bit."

"Were you with Mai-Ling?"

"Sort of, she was talking to this cute guy so I hung back."

"What were you drinking?"

"Bundy and Coke."

"Did you mix your drinks yourself or did someone give them to you?"

"The guy Mai-Ling was talking to got them for us."

She looks over to her partner with a knowing look. As she turns back, her eyes flick to the glass wall behind me. I spin around to see what she's looking at. It's Mai-Ling's mother. As the doctor speaks to her, her sobs become a wail. They take her by the arm and help her up. I try to run out there but the woman cop grabs my arm. Her partner gets up and leaves the room. Mai-Ling's mother is being taken through the plastic doors into the emergency ward.

"I have to go with her. Let me go with her!" My whole body is shaking. I know something bad has happened, something really bad.

"You need to stay here." The constable insists.

"She's my friend. She needs me."

"She needs her mother."

The reality hits. I am just the friend. Even though I'm the one who knows Mai-Ling better than anyone. Even though we shared all our thoughts and secrets, and were there for each other no matter what.

When push comes to shove, I'm not blood, so I'm nothing.

Mai-Ling did need her mother. She needed her more than most but she wasn't like girls our age. While we were all growing up in our flash houses on Sydney's North Shore, she was in Vietnam scraping together money to afford to go to school. I remember when she told me how she came to Australia in a boat no bigger than my father's yacht. Over 20 people including Mai-Ling and her folks crowded together for weeks until they got to Australia. Three people died on the way – one of them was her father. They had to throw his body overboard. If that wasn't enough, when they got here they were thrown into the detention centre at Villawood for three years until, finally, they got a visa and could stay. Her mother has worked 24/7 ever since to give Mai-Ling everything she never had herself. So, yeah, Mai-Ling needed her mum but she had me instead, and that's just life, isn't it?

My head has stopped spinning and now fear runs through my whole body in the place of the pain. The male cop walks back into the room and flashes his partner a strange look. I stand up and push the woman cop's hand off my arm. "I'm going to see Mai-Ling. We're done here!"

I start towards the door, but the constable's stern tone stops me dead. "We will have to do a drug test. You're not leaving until that is done."

I turn back. "You didn't tell me that before. Is that a threat?"

She shakes her head. "We need to make sure you're not at risk."

"Of what?"

"Some serious reaction. Like Mai-Ling's"

"But I'm fine!"

"It's the law."

"What law?"

The guy is shaking his head again and she is giving him a really dirty look. I suddenly get that they can't make me do anything, and she is just pushing me around because she feels like it.

"There's no law. I'm under-age so you'd have to get my father to okay it first, wouldn't you?"

The fog is lifting and I'm starting to think straight. Suddenly I'm wondering why the fuck I'm talking to these two anyway. What possible help is any of this to Mai-Ling? They know what she took, where she took it and the rest is just bullshit. I reckon the guy cop is thinking exactly the same, and it's this stupid bitch who has been watching way too much *CSI* and thinks she's some kind of *who knows what* that's keeping me here.

"So, are you arresting me or something?"

She keeps it up. "No, not at this stage but we do need a blood sample before you go."

I am getting out of my seat now and no-one is stopping me. "In that case, I'm leaving. You want a blood sample? You can wait until my dad gets here and ask him."

As I storm out, I can feel the tension between the two of them. I glance back and they have already started at each other.

Back in the waiting room, suddenly I'm sweating again. The water I drank before has helped but now I am feeling worse than ever. My head is aching and I need to sit down. My legs go to jelly as I reach for a seat. Shit, everything's gone black . . .

I am sitting in one of the plastic chairs but I don't remember how I got here. One of the nurses is taking my blood pressure. She smiles at me as she takes the monitor off my arm.

"Am I alright?"

"It's perfect. You can sit here as long as you need to."

As she stands up I grab her arm, "Mai-Ling, my friend, I came here with her. I need to see her."

She looks at me like she is trying to put a face to a name, "Is she a young Vietnamese girl?"

At last, someone who can tell me what is going on.

"Yes! Can I see her? Is she going to be alright?"

Her face says it all. "Sorry but you'll have to talk to the doctor about that."

"Which doctor? Where can I find the doctor?"

"Your friend is very sick. The doctors are still with her."

"But she'll be okay, right?"

Christ, the look on the nurse's face is horrible. It totally throws me and I start to panic.

"Right?"

I am insisting that she talks to me but she just stares back at me with a prepare-yourself-for-the-worst face. Or worse, that you-have-no-idea-how-serious-this-is face. Oh God, I want to wipe that look right off her face.

"RIGHT?"

I am pleading with her now. I need her to tell me that it is all going to be fine, but she's just staring at me. Tears are streaming down my face as I fumble for the words that I don't want to say.

"She's not going to die, is she?" They tumble out of my mouth anyway. "Is she?" I keep staring at her, "Is she?" Her hand's on my shoulder and she's shaking her head. Jesus!

Slowly, she says, "No-one knows yet. Your friend is still unconscious. The doctor will let you know if there is any change."

She takes her hand off my shoulder and leaves me sobbing. I can feel the eyes of the whole waiting room on me. Oh God, this can't be happening, there has to be a mistake, there has to be . . .

CHAPTER 2

I can't stop crying. I know everyone is watching me but I'm past caring. If there is a God, this is the perfect time for a miracle because I don't know what else will take this pain away. I am wishing that I will wake up and it will all be just a bad dream. I keep imagining that one of those nurses will emerge from behind those plastic doors anytime now and say, "Hey, we got ya! Mai-Ling is fine, but you've both learned a valuable lesson, haven't you?" But I know this is not going to happen and the feeling that I have, this unbearable feeling, is killing me.

Someone has just sat down beside me. I can feel their eyes piercing into my crumpled form, now doubled over on the chair. As I look up, Mai-Ling's mother's face mirrors mine. She's mouthing words but no sound is coming out of her mouth, just tears streaming down her cheeks as her lips quiver.

"Carrie . . ."

My heart is breaking for her.

"Mrs Truong. I'm . . ."

I can't speak either and she doesn't try to make me, she simply nods. We sit in silence for a while before she tries to talk again. "Carrie, they tell me that Mai-Ling might die."

She says this so calmly that I am stunned. "No, Mrs Truong. She's going to be okay." I stammer.

She looks at me like I am the parent trying to comfort the child, and I feel stupid. Her expression is so loving that I know she is not blaming me, even though God knows she should be. I know she wants to say something but she doesn't open her mouth. She stares at me for ages and I'm so confused I don't know what to say to her.

"Mrs Truong I'm . . .

"It's alright."

"I mean, I'm really sorry, I . . .

"I know, Carrie."

Her face is wet with tears and her mouth trembles as she speaks. "Carrie, you're Mai-Ling's best friend."

"Yes."

"You know her. Better than me."

"No . . .

"I knew my little girl once, but not now, not since we came to Australia."

I should take her hand or hug her or something but I can't. She's Mai-Ling's mum, not someone you ever get to know. I only know her the way Mai-Ling talks about her. Not that she is horrible or anything like that; it's just I never think of her as a real person. So instead of hugging her, I blurt out a string of empty words.

"You're her mum. Of course you know her better than anyone."

She shakes her head and covers her face with her hands. "Carrie, I am one woman. I can only do so much and that has not been enough. I have watched her grow from a little girl into a grown woman but I only know the little girl."

"Mrs Truong, I . . ."

"It's alright." She takes her hands away from her face and her bloodshot eyes beg for help. "Carrie, I need to know why. I need to understand the woman my little girl has become. I don't want to lose her, but if I do I will never be able to bear this emptiness inside. Carrie, can you help me to know my daughter again?"

There is nothing I can do to help. Still, I ask, "How, Mrs Truong? How can I help?"

"I want you to tell me about the Mai-Ling *you* know. Everything, leaving nothing out, even if you think I don't want to hear it. Tell me all you know about her, everything you girls did together. Everything." Tears tumble onto her cheeks and her voice breaks into a whisper, "Everything about my Mai-Ling."

I just sit there staring. She is a middle-aged woman who has worked seven days a week all her life. She has no idea of the things I could tell her about her daughter – she would never be able to deal with it. And when Mai-Ling gets better and finds out what I've said, I will lose my best friend. I am like a fox caught in a trap and there is no escape. I think about telling her some bullshit story, enough to stop her questions, but she is staring at me with such sorrow in her eyes that I can't do it. Jesus, I just can't do it! Instead, I nod. She smiles back and softly squeezes my hand. This is going to be the longest night of my life.

———————

So my story begins.

Mai-Ling was pretty shy when she first came to my school. Her English was not great and I guess that's why she ended up in the same classes as me, the low-stream classes. I'm not saying she was dumb or anything, far from it. To be honest, I shouldn't have been in the low-stream either; I was just lazy more than anything else. Oh, and also I thought it was great that my poor performance bugged the crap out of my father. He really hated spending good money on an education that I was seemingly not getting.

He was always writing emails and calling the school, complaining about the "low standard of teaching". He threatened to take me out of there every other week. I reckon they secretly hoped he would so they wouldn't have to listen to his crapping on anymore. That's the thing about my dad, he thinks that money buys everything and solves every problem. He buys me the latest and greatest of everything but he never sits down with me and helps me with my homework. Instead, he works a hundred hour week so he can afford his toys – and his girlfriends.

One year, when I was really little, he organised this fabulous birthday party for me. We had everything; people dressed up like superheroes who were there to entertain us, hundreds of balloons, a jumping castle and all the junk food you could imagine. You name it, we had it. I was so excited and what was really special was that I had my dad to myself for the whole afternoon. He wasn't at work or with a girlfriend or anything, he was with me.

Anyway, just before the party started, he got a phone call. I knew it was one of his girlfriends because of the voice he put on. He has this charming voice he uses when he speaks to women. When he got off the phone he told me that he had to go to work, *an emergency or something. He put on his charming voice for me too when he wanted me to agree with him. He did his usual "I'm-so-sorry-baby-I-promise-I'll-make-it-up-to-you" routine and left. He paid the girl dressed as Wonder Woman to look after me and make sure the party ran well. Can you believe it?*

So, the thing is, there have been so many times when he didn't bother to go out of his way for me that I guess, now, I try to get his attention by giving him the shits. It's stupid, isn't it, but that's how I feel.

That's probably why Mai-Ling and I got on so well when we met – we both had parents who worked 24/7 and this left us with plenty of time to hang out together.

I am suddenly aware of what I have just said and Mrs Truong looks more upset than ever.

"Oh, I don't mean you're like my dad, Mrs Truong. Not at all and neither did Mai-Ling, I swear. I just meant that we were good company for each other because we didn't have anyone at home. Christ, that sounds bad too. I mean . . ."

Mrs Truong is smiling in this understanding kind of way, "It is important to have a good education where I come from. It is the difference between a good life and a poor one. Mai-Ling worked hard on her studies to please me, so 1 could give her that good life. I know she understands that. It's okay, what you have said."

I am in recovery mode now. "That's true, she understands that. I know she does."

She nods and looks down. She tries to hide that she is wiping the tears out of her eyes and I pretend I haven't seen. I feel that I should continue talking as if we were sitting down over a cup of tea or something, to try to ease the tension. But I can't stop thinking about Mai-Ling, and how we had become friends. I push myself to keep going none the less.

We kind of clicked from the start. When Mai-Ling arrived we were in Year 10, our last year of junior school. All the girls in my year had gone through school with me pretty much from the start of high school and we were a pretty cliquey lot, you know. We hung around in groups, the 'popular' girls, the brainy ones, the sluts and the nerds. Then, of course, there were the girls who didn't fit into any group in particular, and drifted from one to the other. I was that kind of girl. No-one hated me but no-one loved me either.

The new girls fell into that group, and that's how Mai-Ling and I got to know each other. We hung around with each other a lot in the end and I suppose it was because neither of us really wanted to be part of any one group in particular.

I look over at Mrs Truong. She seems to have recovered from my last faux pas and is looking at me curiously. I'm not sure what she is thinking but I'm acutely aware that she probably isn't listening to everything I'm saying because I'm prattling on a bit.

"Is this what you wanted me to talk about? Because I can stop if you want."

I am offering her an option to have me shut up but it is really me who wants the out.

She smiles, "Yes, please, go on."

There is no escape; I smile back like I'm happy to keep talking. "Okay."

I continue my story like this . . .

After six months, they moved Mai-Ling up to the top class. It was pretty obvious that she was smart and her English was pretty good by then. It was strange having an empty desk next to me and I began to realise that my shitty attitude with school was making me into a bit of a loser rather than one of the cool kids. And even though my father hated the fact that I was wasting my time and his money I realised that he hadn't made any effort to do anything about it. So I wasn't even getting the attention I wanted. I was wasting my time and no-one else's.

The girls in the higher classes were nicer too. I never would have admitted that before because I was always calling them 'those snotty bitches'. The thing was though, in a funny way being one of them actually felt more comfortable.

Mai-Ling wasn't like that. She was just nice to everyone and people genuinely liked her.

As soon as these words leave my mouth I am conscious of how they sound. I am talking about the past, but in the process I am also talking about Mai-Ling like she is also in the past. I am talking about her like she is a 'was' not an 'is'. Shit, this is not going well.

"Did she talk to you much about school?" I ask. I am trying to get Mrs Truong to talk for a bit. Maybe she might feel better if I let her talk about her daughter rather than listening to me.

"No, I would ask her about it but she shut me out of that side of her life. I thought she wanted to have her privacy but I worried that there was something she couldn't tell me."

Well that worked a treat. Next brilliant idea?

I smile back at her, "Oh."

I couldn't think of anything else to say. There was a lot Mai-Ling couldn't tell her mother. Not because it was really bad or anything, but because her mother would think it was really bad. That's what Mai-Ling would say too. She thought she had to lie to her mother because, if she didn't, she wouldn't be allowed to do anything.

There was also this other thing that happened. Something I did. Something really bad. I know I should tell Mai-Ling's mum but I can't. Not now, not after this.

"Carrie, did Mai-Ling take drugs before this?" Mai-Ling's mum's question interrupts my thoughts.

How do I answer this one? Lie.

"Never. She never did."

When Mai-Ling gets better I promise I'll tell her everything.

"Then why did she take something tonight?"

I don't know why, it wasn't like it was a planned thing or anything. We were just partying. It's not like we're druggies or anything. How do I explain this to Mrs Truong? "I think she thought it was an aspirin."

There is relief on Mrs Truong's face and I'm happy about that, but I feel like crap about lying. The thing is, even if I take my dirty secrets to the grave, at some point Mrs Truong is going to hear something she won't be able to deal with, and that's not going to be something big. It will be something small, something I won't be expecting to be a problem. I know that the more I say the more chance there is of stuffing things up. I'm on the road to Hell without any signposts, and any minute now I'm going to meet Satan himself. Shit! Shit! Shit!

I can see Mrs Truong's mind turning over as she gazes at the floor. "Carrie, do you think it was a mistake, or do you think someone mixed up the tablets on purpose?"

"Probably a mistake."

Christ, give me a break. I'm not good with emotions and I hate it when people cry. I especially hate it when I cry and right now I'm so raw that even talking about Mai-Ling is pushing me to the edge. Why the fuck can't I just be left to sit here on my own? Isn't it obvious how hard it is for me too?!

"Mrs Truong, maybe you should talk to Mai-Ling when she's better. I don't think I . . ."

I am expecting her to push me to continue, or nod, or at least say something. I can't finish what I want to say because I suddenly realise what a selfish brat I am. Mrs Truong is sitting here waiting to see if her only child, her daughter, will live or die. She has sat here and politely listened to me rave on about myself and my problems with my father. She hasn't told me to shut up about myself and talk about Mai-Ling when God knows she probably wants to. She is in pain, and all she has is me to share that with. I am the closest person she has to her daughter right now. I wish I could tell Mai-Ling how lucky she is to have her mum. This thought is killing me because it is beginning to sink in that I might not be able to tell Mai-Ling anything ever again. The image of her covered in vomit on the footpath might be the last image I have of her. Oh God, this is real!

Mrs Truong won't let up about the aspirin. "Carrie, I don't think she thought it was an aspirin. She's too smart, she would know."

"No, I'm sure . . ."

"It's okay. She must have had a reason why she took it. I don't understand it, something must have happened tonight to make her want to do such a thing."

My mind is racing over all the things that I could say to Mrs Truong, but I know she will have no fucking idea about any of it. She wouldn't know the first thing about what guys expect us to do when it comes to sex. How hard it is to stay in the in-crowd, and what it's like to be on the outside for no reason whatsoever. How the pretty girls get the cute guys and the ugly girls get their reputations for being sluts because that's the only way to get a guy. Wrap that up with drugs and alcohol and having a good time. Christ the list is endless and I'm barely able to cop on about it all myself let alone try to talk about it to Mrs Truong. My whole life sucks. It fucking sucks!

"I don't know. We were just talking to people and dancing and stuff. I think it was just a big mistake."

She squeezes my hand. "Thank you for bringing her to the hospital, Carrie. You are a good friend to her."

Christ, how bad do I feel now? I should say to her – no I'm not, I'm the one who's responsible for all of this. It's my fault, my fault. It's all my fault – but I can't. I can't say anything, because if I do I'll cry and never stop.

So instead, we sit in silence.

Mrs Truong stares at the plastic doors at the end of the waiting room for what seems like an age. Her eyes are drowning in tears but she will not let any fall past the lids. This is my entire fault – she knows it and I know it. I feel like shit.

"Mrs Truong, can I get you something? A sandwich or a drink or something?"

"That's okay. Thank you."

She doesn't take her eyes off the plastic doors. It is as if she is willing them to open and for Mai-Ling to walk out into the waiting room. This waiting is unbearable. I sniff back my stray tears and wipe my running eyes.

"Mrs Truong, I really don't know if it will help or make things worse, but if you want me to try to explain where Mai-Ling is coming from, I can. The thing is, I know Mai-Ling in a different way to you, and no offence or anything, but I don't think you'll get some of the stuff and I don't want to . . ."

"I understand. You are young and I am old. We are worlds apart, but she is my daughter and I love her." She is crying into her hands. "I really need you to help me. If she dies, I don't want her to die a stranger to me. Please . . ."

I nod and put my hand on her shoulder. We are past the point of no return. I make a silent promise to her that I will tell her everything, even the bad bits. Even the worst bit. My stomach is churning because tonight, her angel will fall from grace.

CHAPTER 3

Should I start with a positive? You know, talk about something Mai-Ling did which was really cool. The problem is that every time I open my mouth to say anything, I get this terrible feeling like I'm reading her eulogy rather than just talking about my friend.

Christ, I hate myself right now. I have this persistent voice in my head reminding me that Mai-Ling might die. Every time it whispers this thought another voice chimes in with "... and it's all your fault". I can't stop this endless mind-chatter and it's driving me crazy. Mrs Truong is waiting for me to begin my story but I can't start because I'm scared shitless that when I open my mouth all these terrible thoughts will escape and all I'll end up saying is – It was me, Mrs Truong. I killed Mai-Ling! Shit.

And even though there were so many shit-hot things that Mai-Ling did, I doubt Mrs Truong would see them that way. I look like an idiot just sitting here. I need to get my shit together but I'm so all over the place right now. I've got to focus but I can't.

"When we came here . . ." Thank Christ Mrs Truong is rescuing me. . . "Mai-Ling was a happy girl. Even though it was hard on the boat, she never once complained. I knew she missed her friends and I also knew she was scared but I believed it was the right thing to do and it would mean a better life for us in the end."

"Mai-Ling is a really strong person, Mrs Truong. That's why I know she will get through this tonight." That's it, that's my positive. "That's what I noticed about her when she first arrived at our school. So perhaps this is a good place to start."

Mrs Truong is nodding and I've just remembered the perfect story. I'm looking back to when Mai-Ling first arrived at my school, and I'm sure Mrs Truong is genuinely interested when I tell her how I think Mai-Ling found it pretty hard to fit in.

I didn't know her then, so I guess this is just my opinion, but she seemed really out of place. She was in my class but she pretty much kept to herself. No-one really made much of an effort to get to know her either. To be honest, she looked like she wanted to be anywhere else but there and that made her seem like a bit of an ingrate to the rest of us. You know, because she got in on that music scholarship you'd think she would have been really going for it and all. There are heaps of other kids who would have killed for that scholarship.

The teachers tried to get her to answer questions and stuff to help her feel like part of the classes but that just made things worse. She never answered. Instead she'd, like, shake her head and look down at the desk; she never looked up for long from her writing. It took a while before I realised that what she was really doing was trying to scribble everything down by hand. She didn't have a laptop like everyone else.

It's funny isn't it how we assume things about people we don't even know. I thought she was being a bit of an Asian princess, you know, a bit precious. But the truth was that she didn't answer the teachers, or talk to any of us, because she was stressing out trying to write stuff down before class finished.

Mrs Truong is nodding, but I can see from her eyes that her mind is elsewhere. "I would have got her what she needed. I could afford. I didn't know."

"It's okay, it's not like all schools expect the kids to use a laptop so it wasn't like you would necessarily know that." This is a bit of a lie in some ways. If your kid goes to a state school you probably wouldn't assume that you needed to have a laptop. But at the private schools, well let's just say that you would be pretty fucking clueless if you didn't at least think to ask the question.

Mrs Truong is looking at me like she can read my mind. Christ, now I feel like a total shithead for putting her down like that.

She continues nonetheless. "It was hard for Mai-Ling back then because she had spent the last three years in the detention centre. Even though I was her mother, I was no help to her because all I knew was life in Vietnam and the detention centre at Villawood."

And that is the whole problem in a nutshell. I know it and Mai-Ling knows it and it is fucking amazing that Mrs Truong didn't get it until this all happened tonight. Mrs Truong's life is worlds apart from Mai-Ling's. We're not dealing with a generation gap here, we're dealing with a fucking abyss. And the really scary thing slapping me in the face right now is that I am in the exact same situation in reverse.

Fuck, how is it that I never realised this before? I know everything about Mai-Ling's life from the day we met but I have no freaking idea about how she grew up and what it was like to be locked away for years and years. I know sweet fuck all. And here's the twist, I never even thought to ask. I was so busy trying to make her fit in with the whole scene at school that I . . . Jesus . . . I am staring at Mrs Truong and I feel like I am staring right back at myself. Fuck!

Now I am the one who has questions about Mai-Ling and Mrs Truong is the only person with the answers. "I guess we both know half a story each, Mrs Truong. You see, Mai-Ling never talked much about Villawood or Vietnam. It was like she was ashamed of something."

"Your government robbed her of many years; she lost her smile in the time we spent at Villawood. Three years of waiting and every day hoping that the government would decide to allow us to stay. We were treated like we were asking for something we had no right to. We were not born here and so we had to beg for the right to stay."

"That is so unfair," I blurt out because, really, it is. "Why did they take so long? Why couldn't they just let you stay?"

"In their eyes we are like criminals who have come here to take away what they have. They are afraid that we will steal their jobs and their culture. Many years ago, in the 70s they would turn boatloads of people away. Hundreds of people crammed into tiny boats with no food or water left, after weeks and weeks at sea. They would not let them land and there was nowhere for them to go. Many people died. Many, many people. Today, they don't turn us away but they hide us away instead. Then they send us back, one by one, when everyone has forgotten us."

"Jesus, I had no idea, I . . . So how did you get out? Why didn't they send you and Mai-Ling back?"

"We had a friend. A very good family friend, Lun Pham. He helped us."

My heart has just stopped. The mention of Pham's name has made my whole body start to shake. How could she call him a good friend? Is she totally out of her mind or what?

"We knew him back in Vietnam; he helped us find the people who owned the boat we came out on."

I am about to open my mouth and tell her that she has got to be an idiot to think Pham is anything other than a total fuckwit. I want to scream at her and tell her not to bullshit with me. I want to tell her that I know about her relationship with Pham and a whole lot more, but as I open my mouth nothing comes out. The words are stuck like they have tiny bony fingers which are clinging to my lips and won't let go. Mrs Truong has stopped talking like she is waiting for me to say something, but I shake my head. The words at the back of the queue push their way out instead, "Sorry, it's okay, go on."

I close my mouth and she continues.

"Pham travels a lot between Vietnam and Australia but he lives here. He told us that if we came out by boat, the Australian government would be forced to let us stay and that he would help us when we got out here."

"How could he do that? Does he work for immigration or something?"

"He said he knew people who could help and that he would find us a solicitor."

"But it took him three years."

"He never gave up on us. He is a good man."

"No! He's . . ." I can't say it, Jesus why can't I say it? "It's okay, sorry. I mean, It must have been a great feeling to walk out the gates after all that."

Mrs Truong is looking at me like she knows what I really want to say but she doesn't push it, she just keeps talking as if everything she has said is totally true.

"Leaving came with other feelings."

"But they must have been good feelings."
I know I'd be ecstatic if it were me. It would
be like finishing school forever and walking
out the gate for the last time, wouldn't it?

"We had very little money and Sydney
is a very expensive city. My feelings were
happy but they were mixed with worry." I
can tell by her tone that she is giving me
the wind-up on all my questions. "So how
did you and Mai-Ling become friends?"

"Oh, well, Mai-Ling had been at the
school for about a month when the girls
in my group decided they'd had enough
of being ignored. They thought she was
behaving like she was too good for us and
so when they found out you were a cleaner,
well this was enough to . . ."

God, I've done it again. "Sorry Mrs
Truong, it's just that they all came from
families which . . ."

She looks upset but she is tying to hide it. "I understand."

"No truly, wait until you hear the story, Mrs Truong, you'll be really proud of Mai-Ling."

She doesn't look convinced but I continue anyway, and I remember it all really well.

On this day, we were sitting around having lunch when Mai-Ling walked by. My friend, Elle, called her over, pretending to be really friendly. She asked her to sit down with us and introduced everyone at the table.

I could tell she was going to do something really bitchy because she just had that look on her face. You know the one, that really fake nice smile.

Mai-Ling looked uncomfortable but she was smiling and saying hello to everyone. Then Elle moved things up a notch. She asked me what my father did for a living. I glared at her because I could see where this was all going. She wouldn't let up. She was saying, "Come on Carrie, don't be rude. How else is Mai-Ling going to get to know us if we don't tell her a bit about ourselves?"

I answered, you know, saying that he was a solicitor, but I kind of pulled this face like it didn't matter to me what he did. Then Elle went around the other five girls in the group the same way. They had all caught on by now and you could see on their faces that they thought it was really funny.

Mai-Ling said nothing and nodded politely as each girl finished. Then Elle turned to her and asked her what her father did for a living.

She looked upset now and shook her head saying that her father had died. Elle started with this fake sympathy. You know, "Oh, you poor thing. That's terrible." And stuff like that. Then she said, "Well he must have left you with a bit. You know, if you can afford to come to this school."

Mai-Ling shook her head. "No, he didn't have anything to leave."

I was feeling so bad for Mai-Ling. She was fidgeting and looking really uncomfortable but she was too polite to tell them to stick their questions up their arses. Then the big question came. Elle grinned at us like she was about to receive the Nobel Prize for bitchiness and said, "So how does your mother afford to send you to a private school?"

Mai-Ling looked like she didn't even get that she was walking into a trap. She looked as if she was really proud of her mum and said, "My mother owns a cleaning business."

Mrs Truong has started to cry a bit again. "Are you okay, Mrs Truong?"

She wipes her eyes and nods. "Yes, yes, please continue."

"Okay." It's tough, watching her crying like that, but all I can do is carry on talking.

The girls all started to giggle as Elle pushed a little more. "A cleaning business? You mean your mother is a cleaner?"

Christ, I'm feeling like a real bitch just telling this story but what else am I supposed to do?

"I'm sorry Mrs Truong. These girls are real bitches, that's all. It's not . . ."

"It's okay, go on."

Well what happened then was that Mai-Ling answered yes, and the girls started to really laugh. Then Elle says, "I'm sorry Mai-Ling, I had no idea. I thought you would fit into the group but now I'm not sure. I mean, everyone here has professional parents and I don't think we would have anything in common with a cleaner's daughter."

I'm looking at Mrs Truong like I'm waiting to see how she's taking this. But she doesn't move or say anything, so I continue, recounting that moment.

It was horrible; I really felt for Mai-Ling, she just sat there. Then, she did this incredible turnaround. It was a classic; no-one saw it coming.

She said to Elle. "Oh, I think we do have something in common."

Elle grinned at the others, "Oh really? And what would that be?"

Mai-Ling was still putting on this sweet Asian girl voice as she said, "We both know your father has an anchor tattooed on his arse."

It was magic. You should have seen Elle's face: she was speechless. But Mai-Ling didn't stop there, she just kept going. She said, "Yes, I'm sure that it was your father. It was certainly his office. But I only saw his arse as he screwed that skinny young girl on the desk. I've seen her around too; she must work there as well. The door was shut but I opened it because I had to vacuum the office. Anyway, there they were, fucking each other's brains out. So really, now that everyone knows I guess I have something in common with everyone here."

I nearly pissed myself laughing and so did the other girls. All except Elle, that is. She totally lost it, calling Mai-Ling a fucking lying bitch. But we all knew it was true by the way she reacted. Elle had always been so up herself, telling everyone in the group how things were so great between her parents. Especially since most of us had divorced parents.

Mai-Ling was so cool. She got up and walked off as if she had only dropped in for tea and biscuits.

Suddenly Mrs Truong is laughing! Can you believe it; she gets how funny that was. Now I'm the one who's stunned. I thought I'd have to explain to her that Mai-Ling used to see a lot of this kind of stuff when she was cleaning but I guess she knows that. Fuck, you've got to laugh sometimes don't you? Even when things are so shit like they are now.

CHAPTER 4

Mrs Truong is still laughing quietly to herself when a nurse and a doctor burst through the plastic doors. They head towards us and as Mrs Truong gets to her feet, her face turns a ghostly white. The nurse is pointing at us and the doctor is saying something but I cannot hear him over an announcement blasting from the intercom. By the time he reaches us, Mrs Truong looks as if she is going to faint. She is muttering but I don't understand her words; it could be in Vietnamese, I'm not sure.

The doctor is quite young – not much over 30, I'd imagine.

"Mrs Truong?" He is looking at me but I know he doesn't think that I am Mai-Ling's mother. I reach over and help Mrs Truong to steady herself. "Yes, this is Mrs Truong," I say. He's supposed to be a fucking doctor but he doesn't seem to care that I'm holding Mrs Truong up. He doesn't help. Mrs Truong is still gabbling but I don't need to understand the words to appreciate what she is trying to say – she is shit scared. Her face says it all.

The doctor is impatient. Looking straight at me he asks, "Does she speak any English?"

At first I think this is a stupid question and then I think how stupid I am for thinking that. Oh for fuck's sake, what does it matter what I think! "Yes, she does. Is Mai-Ling going to be . . .?"

"We need Mrs Truong's consent to operate on her daughter if it becomes necessary. I need her to sign these forms. Do I need to find an interpreter?"

Mrs Truong is looking at me like she has forgotten the entire English language and I have become her interpreter. "That's okay, I'll tell her."

As I start to speak, slowly and loudly, I become aware that I am treating her like she's retarded. I correct my tone and soften my voice and she suddenly stops her prattling and listens. "Mrs Truong, they need you to sign this form in case they need to operate on Mai-Ling."

Mrs Truong nods as she turns toward the doctor. Everyone goes quiet and I'm about to tell her about the forms again when finally she starts to speak, in English.

"Are you the doctor who is looking after my daughter? Can I see her?"

He doesn't answer; instead he hands her the forms, "Mrs Truong, we need these forms signed now. Your daughter is having seizures and we may have to operate. We need your permission." He is handing her a pen and helping her to sit down again. "You cannot see your daughter just yet but I will let you know the minute you can."

He doesn't seem to care about anything other than his shitty forms. He hasn't asked Mrs Truong if she's okay or if there is anything she needs to know. Nothing. He has told her sweet fuck-all about what's happening in there with Mai-Ling. It's just sign this and shut up. Well, screw me, but that's just not good enough. "Hey, Mai-Ling is her daughter, do you get that?"

He has his signed forms now and thinks that's it, he can go back behind his big plastic doors where it's safe from questioning friends and relatives. No need to talk to the kid's family, he's got what he came for.

Nonetheless he stops and glares at me. "I know that. And you are?"

"I'm her friend. I brought her here."

Christ, you should see the look on his face now. It's like I'm dirt.

"Then, *friend*, do you want me to stay out here talking to you, or would you rather I was back in the Emergency Ward trying to save Mrs Truong's daughter's life?"

Tears are stinging my eyes. This is not how doctors are supposed to be. They are supposed to be caring and helpful, but this doctor is a real dick. He shouldn't be allowed to talk to me this way. The nurse just stands there and says nothing, like she's there as his bodyguard or something.

I try to sound calm but my words are interrupted by the need to gasp in air. "She'll be alright when you operate, won't she?" I am staring straight into the doctor's eyes but he is still dissing me.

"We are hopeful we can release the pressure caused by the bleeding."

"What bleeding?" He is really scaring me now. "Where is she bleeding?"

"I'm sorry, I can't discuss it right now."

He is walking away but I need an answer. "Where is she fucking bleeding!?"

He sighs loudly as he turns to glare at me. "She has haemorrhaging in the brain. If it doesn't stop, we will need to operate. Now, please, let me get back to her."

God, this must have happened when she fell. Mrs Truong is squeezing my hand and I think she is glad that I am still asking all these questions. I know I should just shut up and let them leave, but I'm desperate to know more.

Those voices in my head are back, haunting me like unseen ghosts; my body feels like it is swimming in a pool of guilt. *Mai-Ling didn't hit her head when she fell, Carrie. You know that.* The doctor is retreating towards those plastic doors again and I'm screaming at him. "It's because she fell. That's why she's bleeding, isn't it?"

He stops and turns slowly. I am holding my breath, desperate for absolution.

In a loud voice he announces to the entire waiting room "This can happen with drug overdoses. It's hard to know what was in the pills she took. So no, I don't think it was from a fall."

Fuck! I am still holding my breath and feel as if I will never be able to breathe again. All I can do is stand here and watch them disappear through those doors. *He's wrong!* I scream back at the voices in my head. "He's wrong!" I scream after him and cry into my hands.

Mrs Truong and I are alone again. I should be strong but I can't do this anymore. I can't stand the waiting. The drugs I smoked tonight are wearing off but I've still got this pounding headache and it's hard to think. Everything is way too hard. I feel like I'm poised on a knife edge and any minute now I'm going to be sliced in two.

Mrs Truong is hugging me and holding my head against her shoulder. *I* should be comforting *her* but all I can manage to say through my tears is, "It's okay Mrs Truong.

Mai-Ling's going to be okay, I promise you."
We both know I can't promise that but she
squeezes me in closer like she is thanking
me for at least trying. I feel so useless. "I
should continue with my story."

Mrs Truong whispers like she can keep
this whole thing a secret from the rest of the
waiting room. "You cry first, we can come
back to your story later."

"No, I have to stop crying now." I wipe
my eyes and try to smile. I'm sure it looks
like a try-hard smile but it's the best I can
do. She's nodding and I take that as a yes,
so I calm myself.

Where to start, where to start. I know, I
can pick the story up again a few days later,
after the anchor on the arse episode. Mrs
Truong sits back in her chair as I tell her
about how I was waiting for the train home.
I'd missed the really early one which was no
surprise because I really have to run to catch
that one. Anyway, I was standing on the
platform when I saw Mai-Ling leaning up
against one of the light pillars, smoking.

Christ, here I go again. Too much information! "Shit, you probably didn't know she smoked."

Mrs Truong is smiling like I'm a kid with chocolate all over my mouth trying to deny I've eaten any. "You girls think I don't notice things but I do. I could smell smoke on Mai-Ling's clothes when I washed them. I didn't need to be told."

"Oh, okay. . ." I should have guessed that she would have known. But now I'm wondering if my father knows more about me than he ever lets on. I'm not going to dwell on it though. So I tell Mrs Truong how much it had surprised me back then, because I didn't think Mai-Ling was the kind of chick who would smoke. She seemed like the follow-the-rules kid, you know what I mean?

Anyway, I got this urge to go over and tell Mai-Ling how cool I thought she'd been that day when she'd dissed Elle. You see, Elle was like the leader of the group. Not that we voted anyone as the leader or anything, but she was kind of the one everyone followed. She thought she was pretty shit-hot too, so to see her totally screwed like that it was kind of cool.

Well, seeing Mai-Ling smoking made her seem even more cool. I just wandered over and bummed a ciggie from her. To be honest, I think she was suspicious of me at first and I don't blame her. She handed me the cigarette and turned the other way. I stood there for a bit before I asked her for a light. I didn't really need one because I already had a lighter but I asked her anyway.

As we stood there smoking I broke the ice by telling her how awesome she had been, with her story about Elle's dad. She laughed, saying how the stupid bitch deserved it and, if Elle had continued, she could have brought out a whole lot more about her father's after-hours activities.

I had a new respect for Mai-Ling then. You know, she really knew how to play it. She was fascinating really, and I guess I wanted to get to know her better.

Then just before the train arrived, so did Elle and the others. I'd been sprung, liaising with the enemy but there was nothing I could do, because they had already seen me. They marched over, snotty expressions on their faces and I knew we were in for it.

Elle started with, "So, Mai-Ling, I didn't know you caught the train home. Which one do you catch? The one for all the Westies?"

Unphased, Mai-Ling shook her head. "No, I catch the same train as you, the Hornsby train."

Elle looked at the other girls then back at us, "Well then, let's go. The train's here."

My stomach hit the floor. I knew what a total bitch Elle could be. We got on the train and before we had even pulled out Elle took out these permanent markers and handed one to Mai-Ling.

"So, Mai-Ling, why don't you show us how you do graffiti back where you come from?"

I grabbed the pen and glared at Elle. "That's enough." I felt sick because I knew I'd be out of the group for siding with Mai-Ling but what they were doing wasn't fair and I couldn't stand by and watch.

"What's with you, Carrie? You always put your sign on the carriage. Look, Mai-Ling, it's easy." Elle snatched the pen back and started scribbling something about Mai-Ling on the carriage wall while the other girls sniggered. Then Elle drew a line down the middle of Mai-Ling's white shirt.

She grinned, "Or perhaps Mai-Ling is used to batik prints. What do you think, girls?"

Suddenly they were all drawing on Mai-Ling's uniform. She was stunned and close to tears as she tried to fight them off. The train was pulling into Gordon station so I grabbed Mai-Ling's arm and dragged her off the train. As it pulled out again the others pressed their faces up against the window, laughing and giving us 'the bird'.

Mai-Ling was really upset and ran down the platform crying. I chased after her. She thought I was in on it and wouldn't let me near her. It took me ages to convince her to let me help her to get home. In the end I told her that we could go back to my house and ask my housekeeper, Rosie, if she knew how to get the marks out of her uniform.

She cried all the way back to my place. Rosie had gone and I had no clue how to get the marks out. I tried to rub them out with a damp cloth but it just smudged the marks. She was nearly hysterical about it but I didn't get what was so bad. She could just get another uniform, no big deal really. Then she said that her mum would go totally crazy if she went home like this. She looked really scared . . .

I stop telling my story because I can see the look of shame on Mrs Truong's face. "I'm sorry Mrs Truong, I thought at the time you must have been some sort of dragon lady or something. I guess I was just ignorant, you know, of other people's financial situations. I don't really think . . ."

Mrs Truong is shaking her head, slowly, not looking at me.

"Sorry, Mrs Truong, truly it's not like I think that now or anything; it was just back then."

"That's okay. I understand why Mai-Ling was so upset, but I don't remember her ever coming home with a ruined school uniform."

"I ended up swapping her my uniform and just got dad to buy me another one." It's rude of me I know but since I've brought the subject up, I have to ask. "So would you have gone crazy over it?"

Mrs Truong smiles as if the image of her going nuts is funny, and then shakes her head. "I would have been upset because uniforms cost a lot, but more so because Mai-Ling was being bullied like that. You see, back in Vietnam, the people who had no money were the ones who were treated badly. When we came here, we came with nothing. We sold nearly everything we had to pay our passage on the boat. When Mai-Ling's father died, I was fearful that we had gone through all we had and now we would be no better off. Mai-Ling knew how hard I worked to buy her the things she had. It would have been a difficult thing for her to have to ask me to buy another uniform."

"But it wasn't her fault."

"None of the things which happened to Mai-Ling were her fault, yet she still had to live with the consequences. Life was very hard for us back in Vietnam. In the village, gangs of men would arrive every month and demand money. This money was for protection. Protection, from *them*. Everyone was afraid of them and the few who stood up to them would disappear. For Mai-Ling, these girls would have reminded her of this. It wasn't just the ruined uniform, it would have been the fear that nothing has changed, even here in Australia."

"But it's nothing like that here."

"We sold everything we had to the people-smugglers because we were promised a better life here. We were told that if we arrived we would be allowed to stay. They said the Australian Government would let us stay because of the guilt they felt over turning others like us away, back in the Seventies. But when we came here we had to fight to stay. Mai-Ling learned not to trust but to observe. She saw a different Australia to the one you see."

I am beginning to think that perhaps Mrs Truong is a bit paranoid, or even a bit dramatic. That she could link a scribbled-on uniform to extortion is fucking stupid, if you ask me. I'm not saying what Elle did was okay or anything, but she was just being a bitch and nothing more.

CHAPTER 5

I am sitting in a cubicle in the ladies toilets. I couldn't stay in the waiting room talking to Mrs Truong any longer: I needed to get my head straight. She is probably thinking I have gone home, because I just got up and left without a word. She was still talking about her life in Vietnam but I couldn't listen; it was making things too real. I couldn't listen anymore.

The more she talked the louder the voices in my head were becoming. They wouldn't let up. They kept taunting me with *Carrie, you need to tell Mrs Truong what you did. You have to tell her now.* I screamed back at them to shut up, I'm not even sure if I was screaming out loud or not. I tried to think thoughts over the top of them, thoughts about the fun times I had with Mai-Ling, but it was all too hard. The voices just kept drifting around in my head waiting for me to stop thinking or to stop talking so that I had to listen to them. Fuck!

Memories of the night keep drifting in and out. They are scratching along the inside of my skull and I can't bear them. I hate that I can't remember everything and that I can only remember some things; but most of all, I hate that I have been so fucking clueless.

I can't tell if some of the memories flashing in and out of my mind are real or not. I smoked too much of that stuff they were passing around at the party to be sure of anything right now. But some of the flashes are so vivid, like Mai-Ling screaming at me, and I can't shut them out.

Tonight was just supposed to be fun. That was all Mai-Ling and I went out to do, have fun. Christ, I'm such an idiot; I'm not even sure what I was smoking. My life is so so fucked! It should be me lying unconscious in Emergency, not Mai-Ling. She never took stuff like I did at parties. She always made sure we got home okay, no matter what. But tonight, well, tonight I couldn't get her home. Jesus, I couldn't get her home . . .

Someone has come into the toilets.

"Carrie?"

It is Mrs Truong.

"Are you all right?"

I have to answer because she is sounding so worried. "I'm okay, Mrs Truong. I'll be back out in a minute."

"I will wait for you out here, just in case. I worry about you Carrie."

I want to tell her to go but I really need her to stay. I need someone to help me but I don't know how to ask, and it's like Mrs Truong gets this. I want to cry but she will hear me, so instead I flush the toilet and use the sound to cover blowing my nose with toilet paper, and I wipe my eyes.

As I open the door, Mrs Truong is smiling.

"Carrie, I am glad I found you here. I thought you might have . . ."

"It's okay Mrs Truong. I just needed to go for a minute. Shall we sit back down and I'll tell you more about Mai-Ling?"

"If you are okay to do that. I don't want to burden you anymore."

"You're no burden, Mrs Truong. To be honest it helps with the waiting."

We walk back in silence to our seats in the waiting room. I move on from the 'train' episode. I tell her how, after that, Mai-Ling and I started to hang around a bit. As we sit down I slip back into my story.

I still spent most of my time at school with Elle and the girls, but in the afternoons Mai-Ling and I started catching the train into the city and hanging around there together. It was fun having someone to wander around the shops with. It worked well for Mai-Ling too because she could stay in the city when she was meeting her mum, to help clean offices, and I would just catch the train home.

We were in senior school now and even though it was only our second last year of high school the work was already piling up. To have some sort of distraction I thought it would be cool to have a party at my house before the weather turned too cold. My dad was away on business, so it was perfect timing. Every year I had a party and it was usually the most talked about thing for weeks afterwards. It kind of got me a lot of invites to other things too.

Anyway, I sent out the invitations and included Mai-Ling on the guest list. I thought it would be a good opportunity for her to get to know a whole lot of other people too.

You see it wasn't just my friends who came; everyone invited other people they knew, so there was always a great mix. Mai-Ling was really excited about it too.

Things were going really well, and I had heaps of people coming. Then Elle heard that I had invited Mai-Ling. She was really pissed about this and told me to un-invite her or she wouldn't come.

I had really had enough of Elle and her crap anyway so I thought that it would actually be a good thing if she didn't come. So I told her that Mai-Ling was still invited and she could sort herself out.

It felt good you know, to put Elle back in her box. I hadn't ever really stood up to her before because I always thought she could make my life Hell. This time I thought I had the upper hand for once. I thought that if she didn't come then she would be the one losing out, and if she did come there would be plenty of other people there, so Mai-Ling wouldn't cop shit from her.

It was perfect, and so was the look on her face when I said she could piss off if she didn't like the arrangements. I'd seen the look before; it was one of pure hate and it was always the look she gave people when they'd got the better of her.

Then, a few days later everything came crashing down. Suddenly everyone who had said they were coming started telling me that they weren't coming anymore. Apparently, Elle had a lot more influence than I thought she had. You see, she had boycotted the party and everyone was taking her side. Against me!

I was devastated. I couldn't believe all these girls, who I thought were my friends, were turning on me. Without them I had no party, because they were all bringing other people. I went from being Popular to Try-Hard just like that.

Mai-Ling knew the reason the party was not happening and how upset I was about it. She told me that she couldn't come because she had to help her mum at work, so if I wanted to, I could tell the other girls that I had un-invited her.

I knew that she was lying, that she really wanted to come to the party, but I took the easy way out and made out to everyone that I had told Mai-Ling that she couldn't come.

I am expecting Mrs Truong to give me some sort of disapproving look or make some comment like, *some friend you turned out to be*, but she says nothing. She is just looking at me like she is waiting for me to continue.

If this had been my dad sitting here I would have had trouble getting the rest of the story out, because he would have been spewing all sorts of opinions about what type of person I was becoming. He would have spouted all sorts of platitudes about how I should respect others and not bow to bullies. He'd be so full of shit; and I know that all the advice he'd be happy to dump all over me, he'd never have taken himself.

Mrs Truong, however, is nothing like this. She is simply waiting for me to finish. And of course, there is more to tell.

The party was back on and it was fantastic. At least that's what everyone was saying for weeks afterwards. The problem was, I felt so bad about what I had done to Mai-Ling. She didn't say anything about it, but I knew she was hurt. She sort of got busy after school and stuff, so she couldn't hang out with me. I knew I'd done the wrong thing, but what else was I supposed to do? If no-one had come to the party there would have been no party, and Mai-Ling would have missed out anyway. Christ, listen to me. I am so full of it. Even I don't believe that lame excuse. I think that Mrs Truong is bound to have something to say about that, but as ever she sits in silence, waiting, until I have to speak just to fill the void.

So, then I thought I could make it up to Mai-Ling by buying her something. There was this really cute dress she had tried on in Sportsgirl that cost like $200. I knew she really wanted it, so I bought it for her.

I waited till I saw her at the train station after school and handed it to her, saying that I was really sorry for everything.

I expected her to be really excited and say something like, 'that's okay' or 'no problem', but she just stared at me. Then she let the parcel just fall to the ground and she walked away. I couldn't believe it. I picked it up and ran after her, shouting "What's the matter with you? It was just one fucking party, why can't you let it go?!"

I tried to give her the dress again but she wouldn't take it. I screamed at her that she was a real ingrate, and that if she just opened the present she would see it was the dress she loved, the dress she couldn't afford. The last comment was really bitchy, but I got worse when she didn't stop walking away. So I told her that unless she started making an effort to fit in with the people in this country, she wouldn't be invited to any parties. That she needed to stop with the poor little Vietnamese girl act and start behaving like an Australian chick, and stop being so fucking precious.

Wow. I *had* been a bitch.

"I'm really ashamed of saying all those things, Mrs Truong. I didn't mean it to come out the way it did, but I was so pissed off that she wouldn't forgive me that I just spewed all this stuff at her without thinking."

Mrs Truong is squeezing my hand. "We heard a lot of things like that when we arrived. After a while it didn't matter; we just closed our ears. I think though, for Mai-Ling, it still hurt. But she would never show it. I'm sure she knew that deep down you didn't mean it."

"Oh. Really? But at the time it just made everything worse. Let me tell you what happened."

Mrs Truong keeps hold of my hand as I continue with the story. And I do continue, even though it hurts me to tell it.

As soon as I shut up, Mai-Ling turned around, walked back to me, and took the present out of my hands. Then she said something which totally gutted me. She looked me straight in the eye and said, "If you think an expensive present will make everything alright, then you are mistaken. I thought you were my friend, but friends don't buy each other with presents; they stand by each other, even when it's hard.

"You tell me that you hate your father because he doesn't value you for who you are but right now I am not looking at Carrie, I am looking at Carrie's father. You let yourself be bullied by Elle and your other friends and you turn your back on me. Just like your father, who always chooses to neglect your needs because they are the path of least resistance for him. He lets his boss and his girlfriends tell him where to spend his time, and he leaves you to sort yourself out.

"Then, when you let me down, you think you can buy my friendship back with an expensive dress? How does it feel, Carrie, when your father buys you stuff instead of being there for you? It means nothing, doesn't it!"

She walked off with the present and as she passed the garbage bin on the platform, she threw it away without even looking back at me. It was like she had taken a knife and run it straight through me.

Mrs Truong is still looking at me saying nothing. It is worse than if she was yelling at me and calling me names. I deserve to be called all sorts of things and I could cop it, sweet, but this silence is something else. It is damning. My guts feel like they are being wrenched out of my body with the guilt I am feeling. A guilt which is swamping me, not because of what I have just said, but because I know that by the end of the night she will know everything. And then she will really hate me. Everyone will really hate me.

The fact that my father still hasn't bothered to phone, or come to the hospital, is making me despise him. Mai-Ling was wrong; I'm not like my father. I'm here for her and I'm here for her mum. For Christ's sake, what more do they all want from me!

Mrs Truong finally says something. Her voice is soft and kind. I feel like I want to hug her and beg for forgiveness, but I stay in my seat and listen to her.

"I know that you don't want to be like your father Carrie, but sometimes we have to make choices which make us feel like we are betraying someone else."

"But that's not what I wanted to do. I just felt I had no choice."

"I know. I had something like that happen to me when I was your age, and I still regret it. But it is too late for regrets, so I have to forgive myself."

"What did you do?" I know I shouldn't ask. "Or is it too private?"

"That's okay, I will share it with you."

"You don't have to if you don't want to. I don't want to . . ."

Mrs Truong is not listening to me. She is staring at the ground like she is searching for the right words, and then she starts to speak in a voice which is hardly audible.

"It was when I was around your age and living in Vietnam. I had a sister, two years older than me, who was in love with a boy in the village. My father was strict, however, and he did not like this boy, or the boy's family. He forbade my sister to see him."

"What was wrong with him?"

"My father thought he was too irresponsible and would not be a good provider. The problem was, my sister was pregnant by him, and my father did not know. He told her that if she continued to see this boy, he would throw her out of the family and never speak to her again. In Vietnam, the family is very important. This was a very big threat for my sister and it meant she had a very difficult decision. She had to choose between the boy she loved and her family."

"So she chose the boy, right?"

"No, she chose the family."

"But why? What about the baby?"

"It was a risk if she chose the boy, because she didn't know if he would marry her, and if he didn't she would be left with nothing. She would have a baby and no-one to support her."

"But did he love her?"

"He said he did but that was not enough. She chose the family, but she needed to do something about the baby before anyone found out."

"So what did she do?"

"Abortions cost a lot of money and she had none. She made me swear to secrecy and come with her to the city. She slept with many men that night to get the money, and then she went to see a woman who aborted the baby for her."

"Oh God. That's horrible."

"She was in a lot of pain afterwards and when we got home she was still bleeding. The bleeding would not stop. And she died."

"What about the hospital or the woman, couldn't they help?"

"It was an illegal abortion. It would have brought shame on the family if I had taken her to the hospital. I knew she was in a lot of pain but I took her home instead of taking her to the hospital. I was scared that my father would banish me if I took her to the hospital because it would bring shame on the family. I chose what my father would have chosen, not what I should have done, and my sister died because of it."

I am dumbstruck; I don't know what to say. Mrs Truong's voice is breaking with emotion as she tells me this story. I can see on her face that even though it was long ago, it still haunts her. This time, *I* reach over and squeeze *her* hand and she nods in acknowledgement of this kindness.

Fuck, how she doesn't despise me for having what I have, and still complaining about such tiny details of my life, I'll never understand. Shit.

CHAPTER 6

Mrs Truong is staring at the ground. She has not spoken since she finished her story and I don't know what to say. She blames herself, but what happened is not her fault.

I want to tell her this but every time I open my mouth I feel like a total idiot. I am seventeen years old, what the fuck do I know? Sure there are heaps of things that have happened that I *thought* were really bad but, Christ, it was all just bullshit compared to this. If I tell Mrs Truong it's not her fault, it won't change things. They're just empty words.

I have always taken for granted that if I got myself into trouble, my father would sort things out for me. But I've never broken anything into so many pieces before; never done anything that couldn't be glued back together. Have I done something now which might not be fixable?

All the king's horses and all the king's men . . . the nursery rhyme is like a drum pounding in the back of my mind and, with each beat, a hot wave of fear runs over me. Shit, I don't know what to do.

As I try to bury this feeling, I am staring at Mrs Truong, crumpled over in her seat. She will blame herself if she loses Mai-Ling tonight. She will add this guilt to everything else that has happened to her. No-one will help her because no-one will ever guess what she is feeling. She will just carry on as she always has. She will not see a counsellor or talk about it to friends; it will be her burden to carry alone. As for me, she will thank me for helping her. She will think of me as the friend who was there for her. She will think this unless I tell her the truth. And if I tell the truth I won't be able to hide my secrets away. I will have to tell everyone, and once everyone knows, I can never be "Carrie" again. I will always be despised as "that girl who . . ." Oh shit!

"Carrie?"

Mrs Truong is looking at me now with this caring sort of look. She has no idea how much she is going to hate me. Those voices in my head are taunting me again. The only way I can shut them up is to tell Mrs Truong what I have done. I need her to forgive me to make them go away. I am desperate. "Mrs Truong, I have to tell you something."

She nods, "I know."

How? Pham must have told her something. Shit she has probably known all along. This whole thing is all about making me say it, and Pham has put her up to it! "What do you mean?" I am looking her in the eyes.

"I know you feel bad telling me some of the things that you and Mai-Ling quarrelled about, but you shouldn't worry; they are all part of being friends. You mustn't take the blame for these things. You are a good friend to Mai-Ling and she knows that."

Fuck! Where did that come from? "Mrs Truong, I have something I have to . . ." But I can't, I just can't. "She loves you too, Mrs Truong," I say, knowing that it's lame.

"Thank you."

"Can I get you a drink of water or something?"

"No, I'm okay. I am happy just sitting here and listening to your story."

I nod; at least I can drown out the voices if I keep talking . . .

After the dress thing, Mai-Ling and I weren't friends anymore. I was back with Elle's group, but things weren't the same. You see, Elle always needed someone to ostracise and my turn had come.

She started whispering stuff to the others, looking at me while she did it. When I'd come over to sit down, the conversation would stop the minute I was within hearing distance. You know, all that kind of stupid stuff.

I was determined not to let it get to me, or at least to make it look that way, but it was hard.

Mai-Ling had moved classes too; she was in the top stream now, and she had a whole new group of friends. I had absolutely no-one.

Then it all came crashing down. I was walking past some girls I hardly knew and they started sniggering. I sneered , "What's your problem?" Then one of the girls put her index and middle finger up to her mouth in a V shape and stuck her tongue through it.

As I demonstrate this to Mrs Truong, I am suddenly aware of a woman sitting over by the wall looking at me. My cheeks burn as I snatch my fingers away from my mouth.

Mrs Truong doesn't seem to have noticed the woman. She's just looking at me, "Ah, it means they're saying I'm a lesbian." I feel that I should explain, but the second the words leave my mouth I regret saying them.

I wanted to hit that girl, but I gave her 'the bird' instead, and as I walked away she yelled out, "Give Mai-Ling a kiss from us." I knew exactly who this had come from; Elle. I was determined to have it out with her, but by the time I got to where she was sitting I had been given the same treatment by at least ten other girls. I was totally under attack.

I couldn't take it anymore. I ran into the toilets and cried. I didn't stay at school the rest of the day either; I went home and sat in my house crying. I had no-one to turn to and I was hated by everyone, even Mai-Ling.

Then I did something really stupid. I opened my father's bar and took out a bottle of whiskey. I don't even like scotch but I sat there and drank it anyway. By nightfall I was totally trashed. It was supposed to make me feel better, but all it had done was make me feel a hundred times worse.

I kept going over and over everything from the past few weeks and all I could see was this huge black hole ahead. I hated myself and everyone else and I couldn't bear the way my life had turned.

I was suicidal.

I felt bad and I wanted everyone else to feel bad too. I wanted Mai-Ling to regret not forgiving me for the party thing. I guess I really blamed her for everything that had happened to me and I wanted her to know this. So I texted her a suicide note.

I look at Mrs Truong for some sign of what she is thinking. There is no judgement on her face. As she looks back at me I notice her necklace. It is a really pretty one and

I am surprised I didn't notice it before. I suppose the light has caught it and that is why I have become aware of it. She must wear it a lot because it looks so familiar, but then I hardly ever see Mrs Truong. I shrug this off and keep going on with my story.

It was a crap thing to do, sending that message, but Mrs Truong's face is impassive as I admit to this. I'd actually felt so bad that I'd wanted to kill myself, but when I'd sent that text, I was really just trying to get Mai-Ling's attention. I spent ages composing it, and as soon as I'd hit the send button I guess I must have passed out, because I can't remember much after that.

"Do you ever feel that way, Mrs Truong? You know, really depressed?" It is a stupid question but I am asking because I want to know how she has managed to keep going after all the shit that has happened to her.

"I have felt despair in my life. Overwhelming despair sometimes. So yes, I know the feeling you are talking about."

"How do you get through it?" I need to know how she sits there so calmly when I can feel myself totally unravelling. Having to wait is bullshit. I can't stand it. If I were Mrs Truong I wouldn't be just sitting here waiting to be told when I could see Mai-Ling. I would be screaming and shouting and pushing my way past those plastic doors. I would be telling everyone who tried to stop me to get out of my way and let me see my daughter. But she just sits and waits like she is willing to leave everything to fate. And yet I know she is hurting, I can see it in her eyes. I want to know if this is what happens to people when life slaps them down that once too often? Do they just surrender?

Mrs Truong shakes her head, "There is little choice. You just take each day that you are given and do what you can with it."

"I didn't feel like I could cope with another day, the night I sent that text. I wonder sometimes if I really *could* kill myself. You know, if I ever felt that bad again, could I really go through with it?"

"When you woke up you must have felt differently though, true?"

"Not exactly; that's where my story gets a little twisted."

Mrs Truong looks intrigued, for once, like this stuff about me has really hooked her.

"So what happened?"

Well actually, the text did have the desired effect. I certainly got Mai-Ling's attention alright. Apparently when Mai-Ling got the message, she went into panic mode. She tried to ring me, but of course I was passed out and didn't answer. Then she tried to find out my home number by ringing directory assistance, but they were no help. I was surprised she did this, because I had thought she'd probably just look at the message and think what a total wanker I was. But she didn't, she took it really seriously.

She told me after that she'd even tried to get her mum to leave work early to drive her over to my place but because she wouldn't tell her mum why it was so urgent her mum wouldn't do it for her.

I'm hesitating, wondering if I should tell Mrs Truong this next bit; but I have to, now I've started.

In the end, Mai-Ling called Pham and convinced him to pick her up and drive her over to my house.

Anyway, when they got there the back door was unlocked, so Pham waited outside while Mai-Ling went in. She said that she was terrified she would find me with blood everywhere, dead on the floor. When I think back it must have been really hard to even come inside the house, expecting to find that. I'm not sure that I would have been able to do it.

When Mai-Ling found me passed out on the bed, she was furious with what I had done. I woke up to her hitting me and shouting all sorts of things. I couldn't figure out what was wrong with her, because I had forgotten all about the text.

She was screaming that I was such a bitch for putting her though this, and that she had come through the back door expecting to find a dead body. Then she started crying, like people do when they are really distraught. She sat down on the bed next to me, and hugged me while she bawled her eyes out.

It took ages for her to calm down. I thought she would never forgive me, but for some reason she did. It was like everything that had happened before was all forgotten, and in that moment we became best friends again. I never got why she had got so upset about the dress thing, and yet this shit that I had laid on her, which was a hundred times worse, made us close.

Mrs Truong nods like she totally understands. She has pursed her lips like she is ready to say something important.

"There is a reason Mai-Ling was so upset with what you did."

It will be my fault, I know it, so I might as well apologise again and get it over with. "I know, it was a shit thing to do to someone, and I'm really sorry."

She continues like she has not even heard what I have just said. "In Villawood, a friend of Mai-Ling's hung himself. He was fifteen. They would spend hours talking, but one day she couldn't find him and went looking for him around the compound. He had hung himself with his bed sheet. It was Mai-Ling who found him."

"Oh my God, she never told me this."

"She was devastated. He was her best friend and he never even hinted that he would do such a thing. For many months after that, she became withdrawn. I thought I would lose her the same way, but then we were granted our residency. I think that was what saved her."

"Why did he do it?"

"The children in the centre had very little to do. There was nothing to keep their minds active. I believe he lost heart, and with that, he lost everything."

"I'm so sorry Mrs Truong." I mean that, too. I have spent my whole life demanding that people love me. I wish I were someone else, anyone other than who I am, because the person I am is so pathetic. But I at least have hope, and no-one has taken that from me.

Mrs Truong's necklace catches my eye again and it suddenly hits me where I have seen it before: it's exactly like the necklace my father's girlfriend accused me of taking. My God, I can't believe Mrs Truong has one the same. I have to ask. "Your necklace, it's really pretty. My father's girlfriend had one like it."

Mrs Truong puts her hand on the small cluster of diamonds which are hanging from the chain. "I love this necklace. Pham gave it to me for my birthday."

As she says this I am suddenly seeing another piece of the puzzle. Pham must have taken the opportunity to rob the house while Mai-Ling and I were . . . Fuck! It never occurred to me to wonder what happened to him that night, because he had gone by the time Mai-Ling was ready to leave. What a prick!

I am so angry. I am so angry that Pham has got away with so much. He thinks he can take whatever he wants: things, people – anything. When he doesn't want it anymore, he just throws it away like it never meant anything anyway. Mrs Truong thinks he loves her, and you can really tell, the way she fingers that necklace. She thinks he is the one person in this world that she can trust. Fuck, I am so pissed that he gets away with murder like that.

I need to make Mrs Truong understand who Pham really is. She needs to know that he is not her friend; that *he* is the one to blame for everything. That necklace is nothing to him. It is a shiny thing, a distraction from the truth. It is not love, it is an illusion. And what's worse is that by trusting Pham like she does, Mrs Truong is hurting so many people, and she has no fucking idea about any of it. I want and need to 'out' the prick, but how can I without confessing my own part in the dirty lie? God I hate him!

She takes her hand away from the necklace.

I bite my lip and say nothing.

CHAPTER 7

We have been waiting for two hours now, and still no-one tells us what is happening with Mai-Ling. Occasionally, a doctor pushes through the plastic doors and both Mrs Truong and I hold our breath as we brace for bad news. But each time, those doctors hurry past. Neither of us speaks when this happens; it is as if we are both afraid to give life to our fear. The waiting room is full again; all seats are taken except those on either side of us. We are castaways on an island in the middle of this sea of people. I'm not sure why we are being given this communal snub, and care even less. Waiting is like a slow death. Like we are insects caught in a web, struggling to escape but preparing for the end. Has it been too long to hope for good news? I can't convince myself any more that things will be alright. I'm hoping that when someone finally speaks to us we will not be told the worst.

Every time a doctor disappears into the catacomb of corridors, I promise myself that I will crash-tackle the next one and hold them down until they tell me exactly what is going on. But each time one of them pushes through those doors I freeze, shit scared that if I ask the question, I will be told the answer. I stay in my seat with my lips pressed together.

"Did Mai-Ling have a boyfriend?"

I sit bolt upright. Not because the question is hard to answer, but because it catches me off guard and sets those voices off again. Christ, they are screaming at me, taunting me to answer that question with all kinds of shit. *Ask her, go on; ask her to define the word 'boyfriend'. Ask if she means the type of boyfriend who takes you out on dates and stuff, or the kind of boyfriend Pham is to her. You know, the kind you keep secret, and just screw now and then.*

All this shit is blasting away in my head and I can't reply to Mrs Truong's perfectly reasonable question in case I come out with these awful thoughts. I can't get past how fucking pissed off I am with Mrs Truong right now either. If she wasn't so fucking stupid, none of this would ever have happened. If she had just opened her eyes and seen what a creep her 'hero' Pham is, then Mai-Ling would have been able to answer this question for herself. For fuck's sake, I want to blame Mrs Truong for everything, and the voices are insisting if she hadn't been screwing Pham, none of this would have happened. *Tell her, go on, tell her!* Shut up! Shut up!

I don't want to be like this, like some kind of judgemental bitch. I just want to forget everything that has gone on and go back to the way things were. Way back, before everything got so out of control.

I'm shit scared of my own thoughts. A war is going on inside my skull and I feel like I'm going crazy. Christ, is this how I'm going to be from now on? Is this it? Am I going to become one of those weirdos, pacing the streets muttering and mumbling and yelling abuse? Shit, what if I'm already like that and I just haven't noticed? What if the few drugs I have taken at parties really *have* rewired my brain and I just can't see . . .

I am sucking in air and holding it as long as I can to try to stop my mind racing, but Mrs Truong has assumed that I'm upset again because of Mai-Ling. She touches my shoulder and looks at me, like she knows how I feel. "It's alright Carrie; you don't have to tell me."

She is so nice; too fucking nice to me, and I'm such a bitch in return. Jesus Christ, Carrie, answer the woman's question!

"It's okay Mrs Truong, I was just thinking."

"I know Mai-Ling probably has a boyfriend; I guess all girls your age do."

"Actually no. Mai-Ling doesn't have a boyfriend anymore. But she did last summer."

"She never said. Was he a nice boy? Was he good to her?"

Christ, define good! "They had a good time together. We all had a good time together actually. I can tell you about it if you want."

"Yes, I would like to hear."

"Okay, well do you remember when Mai-Ling stayed with me at my place, when my father was in Europe? That's when it all started."

I am glad to be telling Mrs Truong about a time which was totally awesome. I can see that she is glad to hear something good too. So I tell her how great it was to have the whole house to ourselves, and no-one to tell us what to do.

We spent loads of time at the beach just hanging out with surfies and there were so many parties. You know, impromptu ones, where we'd all go to the city for a while, then end up at someone's house and spend all night just talking and listening to music and stuff.

Alex was this really cute surfer we met at the beach. I could tell he liked Mai-Ling; he was always looking at her and doing stupid stuff in front of her. You know, making smart comments or throwing her over his shoulder and not letting her down, even though she was squealing and begging him to. Just fun stuff.

Mai-Ling thought he was cute too, and loved the attention. She'd talk about him all the time but she wouldn't go over and ask him out. She was way too shy to do that. There was this other girl, Kirsten, who liked him too, and she was all over him. To be honest I didn't understand why he didn't tell her to piss off because it was obvious he thought she was a bit of a dog.

One night, we decided to stay in and just watch DVDs and stuff. We were curled up on the lounge in our pyjamas, eating pizza, when Mai-Ling got a text message. She was so excited when she saw it was from Alex. All he'd written was, "where r u?" but Mai-Ling was nearly wetting herself over it, like he'd asked her to marry him or something.

I told her to wait for half an hour before she texted him back, but after five minutes she couldn't help herself. She was going to write something stupid, like the truth, so I grabbed her phone and texted for her, "out with Carrie". I told her that the last thing she wanted him to know was that we were just hanging around at home.

It seemed ages before he replied. Mai-Ling was checking her phone, like a million times. We had almost given up when she got another text, "can i meet up with u?"

You should have seen us; we flew into the bedroom and started dragging clothes out of the wardrobe, throwing on make-up and fixing our hair. It was madness really but we had to keep up the story.

We met up in the city about an hour later. Alex brought a mate along and I spent most of the night talking to him, so that Mai-Ling could have Alex all to herself. Then Mai-Ling dragged me into the Ladies and said we had to go home. I didn't get it, but we left anyway, because she was really insisting.

Anyway, later on she told me that he had asked her to go back to his place with him, and that's why she'd wanted us to take off. I didn't realise that Mai-Ling was still a virgin, and if I had I might have understood her a little more. But as it was, I was like, "What's the matter with you? You think he's really cute and he's obviously really into you, so why didn't you go home with him?"

I didn't think he'd call her back, but how wrong was I? He started texting her before we even got home.

Mai-Ling was so cool after that. She had a really cute boyfriend and everyone knew it. Alex was a nice guy too. He really respected her, even though she wasn't sleeping with him or anything. That's kind of unusual I think, for a guy to still hang around with a chick he's not getting any from. Anyway they were like, together all the time for the next couple of weeks and Mai-Ling was really happy.

Then Alex stopped seeing her so much and Mai-Ling started to get all insecure. I tried to tell her that guys like to spend time with their mates, and not every minute with their girlfriend, but she didn't believe me. She was convinced she had done something wrong. From then on every text she got I had to analyse for 'signs', interpreting each one for hidden meanings. She was sending me mental. I think it was then that she started to think that maybe he was seeing someone else because she wasn't sleeping with him. It had crossed my mind too but I didn't say that to her.

They had only been going out for like a month, and she was acting as if they'd been together for years. She started all this stupid girl shit, like holding off on making plans with me in case Alex called. And she was constantly checking her phone and stuff, in case he'd left a message. I was really getting the shits, especially since she was still seeing him a couple of times a week. It wasn't like he'd dumped her or anything.

Anyway, one night we were all going out in a big group and she told me on the bus on the way there that she was going to go home with him that night to, you know, have sex with him . . .

Shit, Mrs Truong's face says it all. Fuck, I thought she would have assumed that Mai-Ling had had sex. Fuck! I've done it again.

"Mrs Truong, it's not like she was a slut or anything. Everyone does it, you know? It's okay." Mrs Truong's smile looks forced and I know she's not handling this at all. "Are you alright, Mrs Truong? I'm sorry I told you, I should have kept my mouth shut,

I'm really sorry."

Mrs Truong is nodding slowly, like she's processing everything over and over again. "Did she go home with this boy?"

This is my out, and I should take it. I should say, "no" and pretend like Mai-Ling had decided to wait for her wedding day or some shit like that, but I can't carry it off. She'd know I was lying, so here goes. "Yes, she did."

Mrs Truong is just looking at me like I haven't finished my sentence, but that was all I was going to say. Jesus, what am I supposed to say? "And she was really glad she did." Christ why did I say that? "That's what she told me anyway . . ." I'm not making it sound any better. "Anyway, that's what happened." *Please, please don't ask me any more!*

I'm expecting Mrs Truong to cry or get mad or something, but she's not. She's actually smiling, almost like she's okay with it. Go figure. She takes my hand and squeezes it.

"Carrie, I am glad she did that. I'm glad she enjoyed."

"Pardon?"

"I'm glad that she enjoyed sex, and I'm glad that she can choose who she sleeps with. I could never speak to her about that sort of thing. I didn't know what to say. But I know if we had stayed poor and in Vietnam, she may not have been able to choose for herself. She may have had to make a decision based on security, not her feelings. So I am glad."

Oh my God. Mrs Truong blows me away sometimes.

"So what happened to this Alex?"

Now comes the bad news. "Oh, he dumped her a few weeks later."

"Dumped?"

"He didn't want to go out with her anymore."

"But Mai-Ling gave him her . . ."

"I know. She was really hurt by it. She was crying for days and kept going over and over everything they did, trying to figure out what she'd done wrong. I tried to make her see that it wasn't any big deal, that he was just one guy. You know, there are heaps of cute guys out there, it's not like she couldn't get another boyfriend or anything. Don't buy the book when you can borrow the whole library, that kind of stuff. But it still took her ages to get over him."

I can see that Mrs Truong doesn't get what I'm saying, and now I'm starting to realise something that *I* didn't get until now, either. I am starting to think that Mrs Truong is not actually in love with Pham after all. It's like a duty fuck for her. Payment for everything he has done for her. Shit! She's not left her old life behind at all. And here's the really fucked-up part: she thinks Mai-Ling *has*.

CHAPTER 8

Every time I ask Mrs Truong if she needs something to eat or drink, she says no. I have asked her like four times, and the answer is always the same. I realise she is just being polite, so this time I haven't asked, I have jumped up and gone looking for the canteen.

Not that I'm being totally selfless; I'm starving. The thought of eating, up until now, has been disgusting. My stomach has been too churned up to even consider it, but I have finally come down off whatever it was I smoked, and now all I can think about is eating something fast.

I buy sandwiches and bottled water at a shop just down the corridor. Back on our little island, I have this crazy image of us breaking out the picnic rug and sitting down to eat. I smile to myself but it's too silly to share with Mrs Truong. She is grateful for the food, and I feel that I have managed to do something right.

We eat without a word but I see a look from Mrs Truong like she can't quite put something in its place. I brace for more questions.

"Carrie, I thought you and Mai-Ling were in the same classes, but now I remember, she moved to the A stream at the beginning of the year."

"She did, and I was left behind in the lower classes. I managed to move up, but that's another story."

She looks at me expectantly. "Actually, a whole bunch of things happened at the beginning of the year with me and Mai-

Ling, but it's not the kind of stuff you want to hear about."

"We have come a long way on this journey together tonight. I know you have found it difficult to say some of the things you have said. I am grateful for this, and if you can share more, I would like to hear."

I take a deep breath, brace myself and say, "Okay." I plan to give Mai-Ling's mum the edited version, but as I start telling the story, I end up blabbing the whole lot none the less.

As I remember it, Mai-Ling was only taking basic maths, science and English for her senior years, and this meant that she wasn't going to get the kind of marks she wanted in the Higher School Certificate. It's all about weighting and stuff so even if she did brilliantly at these levels she would only be ranked the same as the kids who did okay in the top levels.

When she started the last year of junior school I don't think anyone really explained that to her, and when she asked to move into the higher streams, the teachers weren't very keen to let her. This was the first time I'd ever seen Mai-Ling stand up and fight. She took it to the principal in the end, and he agreed to let her move. It meant she had a lot of catching up to do but she really knuckled down and started studying hard. So much so that I hardly ever saw her after school or at the weekends any more.

After such a fun summer, I really felt left out and alone. The crowd I used to hang out with, Elle's group, were not my friends any longer and I really had no-one else. It dawned on me, too, that I wasn't going to get great marks in the final exams, you know, the HSC, either if I stayed where I was. All in all, my slack attitude was only serving to piss my father off, but it wasn't going to help me in the long run. So I decided to take school seriously and get into the higher stream as well.

It was great to have Mai-Ling to study with; we worked really hard after school, catching up and getting through the assignments. There was a mountain of work, but for the first time I felt motivated to do well, and it showed in the marks I started getting.

My father noticed the change and I thought he'd be proud of me. But instead of giving me the credit for making such a big effort, he gave himself a big kissy-poo up the arm for being so insistent with those stupid letters he kept sending. You know, the letters to the school where he complained about how he was paying a shitload of money for my education and how it was their fault that I was failing. What a wanker, he thought he was so great because he had forced them to smarten up their teaching standards. Can you believe it?

Anyway, at the end of Term One we had all these assignments to hand in, which went towards our final marks. The HSC assessment means you have to do well throughout the year, as well as in the final exams.

There was this English essay that was worth like twenty per cent of the assessment, and Mai-Ling and I spent weeks working on it. We each did our own work, but we would, like, read bits out to each other along the way, to see if it sounded okay and that kind of stuff.

Just before the essay was due I got the flu and was really sick for days. I had finished the essay, so I was going to email it to school. Anyway, Mai-Ling rang to see how I was, and offered to hand it in for me. So, long story short, I emailed it to Mai-Ling instead.

A few weeks later the marks came back and my mark was pretty good, but Mai-Ling's mark was fantastic. She had topped the year with it.

We were both so excited, especially since English wasn't her strong subject. Then later that week I got a total shock. Mai-Ling was asked to read her essay out to the class, kind of to show us what we should aspire to in the HSC. She didn't want to, and I thought it was because she felt self-conscious reading aloud. The teacher offered to read it instead, but Mai-Ling still objected. In the end the teacher asked another girl to read it out, and when she started the first sentence I couldn't believe what I was hearing. It was my essay! I pulled the essay I had supposedly handed in, out of my bag and realised that the first two paragraphs were similar to mine but after that it was Mai-Ling's essay.

Mai-Ling wouldn't look at me, and when the bell rang she got up and disappeared before I could say anything. I was so angry. I had worked just as hard as she had on the essay, and for the first time in my life I had done really well at school. And no-one knew it!

When I finally caught up with her, Mai-Ling was crying and saying how sorry she was. I couldn't believe she'd done it. I trusted her above everyone. I started screaming at her about what a bitch she was, and how I was going to prove that it was my essay, and her crying became hysterical. She was screaming back how if I did that, her mum would punish her really badly and she'd lose her music scholarship and have to leave the *school. She went on about how I had heaps more opportunities to get ahead and she had none and I would be taking everything away from her if I told.*

What could I say after that? I felt like shit and I was really angry – so angry that I slapped her, I felt so betrayed. Right away, I regretted it. Mai-Ling looked totally shocked as she stopped screaming, and she just stared at me. I was saying sorry, like a million times, but she just kept staring. Then she walked away from me the way she did that day at the station, you know, with the dress thing. I ran after her, but she wouldn't talk to me. She totally dissed me and I found myself promising that I wouldn't tell. By then I was almost begging her to forgive me. How things got turned around like that I can't say, but I really felt like I had to make-up with her.

I am telling Mrs Truong this the way a little kid tells tattle-tales to another kid's mother. In some weird way, I guess I am thinking that Mrs Truong will apologise for Mai-Ling, like some mums do. Oh fuck, her face is shiny with tears and now I feel even worse. Pretty soon, I am back in recovery mode.

"Mrs Truong, I know why she did it; I was just surprised, that's all."

I feel totally ashamed. She's got enough to deal with right now, and here I am, dumping my shit on her. What's worse, Mai-Ling is not even here to defend herself, so I'm, like, ratting on her behind her back. I've hit a new low and it feels totally fucked. The thing is, even if Mai-Ling had done something a hundred times worse it will never be even close to what I have done to her and here I am acting like I'm Mother fucking Teresa.

Now the tears are washing down my face; am I ever going to get past all this guilt? Everything is so messed up. How the fuck am I expected to deal with this sort of shit? I can't face Mrs Truong crying and I can't face myself either. Where the Hell is my father? He's supposed to be here; he's supposed to be fixing this whole mess up and he hasn't even bothered to call. Who am I kidding? It's not like he's ever given a shit about me, the prick. And yet here I am, sitting with Mrs Truong, who in the last few hours has offered me more support than my father has in a lifetime, and I'm shitting all over her. And worse is yet to come because I don't know if I can keep this secret forever without going crazy. And even if I do manage to and everything turns out alright because Mai-Ling gets better I'm still up Shit Creek because then Mai-Ling will tell her mum what I did. Then Mrs Truong will see me for what I am, an evil little lying bitch. They will both hate me and I will never be forgiven. I will never be forgiven for making one stupid, stupid mistake.

Mrs Truong is sobbing into her hands and everyone in the waiting room is staring. They are blaming me, thinking that I've made her cry, and they are right. I can't even pretend that I didn't want to tell her this bit of the story, because I did. In a sick and twisted way I wanted Mai-Ling's mum to know what she did because deep down, I am still pissed off about it. It's like

I can't stop at just one slap, I have to keep on hitting. I keep striking out at everyone who's nice to me, while the people who are supposed to love me – like my father – get away with everything. I don't say or do anything to them. I just cop it sweet and make everyone else pay.

"Mrs Truong, it doesn't matter about the essay. I don't care about it and I understand why Mai-Ling did it. If I'd been in the same situation, I would have done the same."

Mrs Truong is shaking her head, "No Carrie, I am ashamed at myself for not telling you something."

"It's okay," I interrupt her. "I know you wouldn't have gone off at Mai-Ling for not getting the top mark. I know that now. You don't have to explain anything."

"No Carrie, I do. I have sat here for hours now letting you believe something that is not true. I have said nothing, and let you blame yourself for things which are not your fault."

"But . . ."

"Please, let me finish. I know you think that Mai-Ling has a music scholarship, and that is how her school fees are paid. But this is not true."

"It's not? Then how . . ."

"Pham pays for everything, including her schooling, in exchange for something from me."

Oh my God, she's going to tell me she's a hooker and I'm not going to be able to hide my reaction. Oh shit.

"Carrie, you know I own a cleaning business."

She's going to tell me it's really a brothel. Shit, shit, shit! "Yes . . ."

"Well, in exchange for Mai-Ling's school fees, I allow Pham to launder money through my business. Big money. Drug money."

"Fuck!" The word flies out of my mouth before I can stop it.

"If Pham knew I was telling you this it would be very dangerous for both of us, so I beg you to say nothing. My family owes him a great debt and if we don't pay, he will cause trouble. Much trouble. We could even be sent back to Vietnam."

"Oh, Mrs Truong, I had no idea."

"I know. I am only telling you so that you understand why Mai-Ling did what she did. She must do well at school or Pham will be very angry. He loves Mai-Ling like a daughter and expects her to make the most of her opportunities. He is not a cruel man. He does what he does out of love and respect. I know from where you sit it is hard to understand, but it is our way. Education is the most important thing of all. It is the thing that can lift you out of poverty."

My mind is racing, searching for a clue that Mai-Ling knew this. I can find nothing.

Everything she said and did seemed totally transparent, but now I feel like I really didn't know her at all. It was stupid to think that she could just have taken her old way of life and shoehorned it into a new one here, without some tearing at the seams.

And now it is making sense, why Mai-Ling was screaming so hysterically at me earlier tonight. Why, when I started throwing stuff at Pham's car and shouting at him to fuck off out of Mai-Ling's life, she was dragging me back inside and begging me to stop. I thought I was protecting her, but Christ, I was making things a hundred times worse for her. And a hundred times worse for Mrs Truong. And then a million times worse for everyone, because of what I did after that! God, I'm going to have to face up to that now. And Mrs Truong will have to be told. Oh God!

"I have to go to the toilet." I can't even look at Mrs Truong as I jump out of my seat and run down the corridor. My tears sting my cheeks as they fall and I am desperate to find somewhere to let them flow freely; somewhere where no-one will see me cry.

I slam the door of the cubicle and collapse onto the toilet seat.

CHAPTER 9

I have been sitting in this toilet cubicle for what seems like ages but is only about fifteen minutes. Mrs Truong has not come looking for me and I wonder whether this is a bad sign. Maybe she thinks I am cross with her because of what she said. She probably thinks a lot of things that are equally untrue but what can I do to change that? Her view of the world is so screwed-up that to try to make her see things differently would be like trying to untangle a ball of barbed wire – painful.

I will go back out there soon. I just need a few more minutes of peace; time to think, that's all I want right now. Not much, just enough to figure out how I am going to sort this mess. Aunt Liz used to say to me, "Don't sit there whinging because that won't change anything. You've got two choices with every problem. Fuck it or fix it. It's as simple as that." Yeah right. Well then, my friend, I certainly have fucked this one!

Now for my next trick. What will it be? To go back out there and keep telling my story to Mrs Truong? Or sit there with her, pretending that everything is going to be okay? Christ, we both know things are seriously wrong. So how long before one of us cracks and actually says it out loud?

My feet are taking me back to the waiting room. It is as if they have a mind of their own. Or maybe they are so over listening to all my bullshit. Either way, I give up and tag along.

Mrs Truong is right where I left her but as I walk towards her I am shocked by how old she looks. It is like she has aged twenty years or something in the last few hours. Her face is drawn and lined and she looks like she has given up on everything. I hand her a coffee and she smiles up at me.

"Sorry for leaving you like that. It wasn't about what you said or anything. I just . . ." Shit, now I'm crying. "I'm sorry . . ." Jesus, she has stood up and is hugging me. I'm not the huggy type but I am hugging her right back. The whole waiting room is probably looking at us but I don't care. I ask in a shaky whisper, "H-have they said anything more about Mai-Ling?" Mrs Truong's face falls and her eyes water as she shakes her head. I want to sit down again but I don't want to offend by being first to break away. That's why I don't like hugs. Everyone seems to always hang on for ages and I never know how long before I can pull away. She has read my mind again because she has dropped her arms. We sit and I take this as a chance to start to make things right.

"Mrs Truong, I want to tell you about a big fight Mai-Ling and I had and about something I dared her to do. Maybe then you'll see why we are so close, not because I want to tattle-tale or anything."

She sips her coffee and nods, "I don't think you are telling tales. I know how much you care about Mai-Ling. Please, go on."

My respect for her is growing. I mean she is so decent, exactly like a mum *should* be. Mai-Ling is lucky to have her. And I always thought I had it good because Dad had so much money. Go figure.

Anyway, here I go again. We shift around on the hard plastic chairs and settle in for the next episode of my story.

Halfway through this year we did our Trials, you know, the practice exams for HSC. Mai-Ling and I had really worked hard and I felt pretty confident that I would do well. I had the advantage because I was better at English. By this time I had kind of forgiven her for the essay thing and we hadn't spoken of it again.

I was part of a new group of girls too and had even regained some of my popularity as one of the cool chicks. But Mai-Ling was also pretty popular too and there was an unspoken rivalry between us.

The problem was, with this new crowd I kind of felt like I was 'the friend'. You know, like I was included because I was with Mai-Ling. Unlike when I was part of Elle's group; then I was the popular chick and Mai-Ling was the nerd.

Deep down I felt a bit insecure so I started to compete with Mai-Ling over silly things. I knew if I beat her in the exams this would really mean something. I would have some kind of edge, you know? It was like my new gang would rate me more than Mai-Ling because I was smart, that kind of stuff.

Anyway, I thought I would be able to shrug it off if Mai-Ling did better than me; that I was cool enough to not let it affect me. But when the results came back and Mai-Ling had topped the year, I couldn't handle it. I knew she got better marks partly because of my essay. Suddenly I was back in that space again and couldn't let it go.

I hated being so shitty but I couldn't help it. Everyone was congratulating Mai-Ling and the teachers were gushing over her like she was a genius. She just lapped it all up like she really deserved it. She could have said something like I know my marks were better because of your essay and thanks for not saying anything. At least I'd have felt she appreciated what I had done, but she said nothing.

I stopped hanging out with her to punish her. I never discussed it with her; I just stopped speaking to her at all. It worked too. I could see it really hurt her feelings and she didn't know what she had done. She'd like, try to call my mobile and stuff but I'd reject the call. Then she'd text me but I'd never reply. It was really bitchy but I didn't care.

In the end she was so desperate to be back as my friend that she chased me all the way to the train station to talk to me. I was really stand-offish with her and she ended up crying, which I kind of thought made up for the way I felt but I didn't let her off. She was standing on the platform with everyone staring at us, going on how she was sorry for whatever it was that she had done. I told her that she was a fraud and a cheat and her marks were bullshit. As soon as she figured out I was still going on about the essay thing, she changed. She stopped crying and got really mad. She like started screaming, "When will you get over that? I said sorry like a million times. What do you want me to do about it now!" I said that if she was really sorry she had to prove it to me. That she had to do something that I dared her to do. It was cruel and I hate myself for doing it but I wanted her to make a sacrifice for me so I dared her to shoplift with me.

I wait for a reaction from Mrs Truong but she just asks another question as though what I'd requested was perfectly reasonable. I am getting used to this type of response from her now and it is okay really.

"So what did she do, Carrie?"

"I didn't think she would but she did and then . . . well I'll explain what happened."

We went to Myer department store and stuffed a pair of sunglasses under our jumpers when we thought no-one was looking. Mai-Ling looked kind of nervous but I was pretty cocky. I'd done it before and got away with it so I figured it was just a bit of a joke really to see Mai-Ling take it so seriously.

Anyway, on the way out of the store this security guy stops us. I was totally taken by surprise. I hadn't spotted him watching us but he even knew what the sunglasses I had taken looked like. When I tried to deny I had them, he made me put my hands up and they fell out from under my jumper. I looked at Mai-Ling who was made to do the same but she had nothing. I couldn't believe it; somehow she had managed to get rid of them before we got caught.

They let her go but I was marched back into the store where they wrote down my name and stuff and called Dad. He had to come down and get me and he was so pissed off. In his mind he was such a tough love kind of father and made up this really lame punishment to make me regret what I had done. He grounded me for a month. Can you believe it? Stupid old fart. I didn't care because he was never home anyway, so he had no idea whether I was there or not.

There was a time when I would have been pissed off with Mai-Ling too for leaving me to take all the blame. But actually, I thought she was pretty cool for being smart enough to ditch the stuff. I had this new-found respect for her and we were so back to being friends again.

Funny isn't it? I was shitty because people thought she was smarter than me at school but really impressed that she was better than me when it came to stealing. It's nuts really.

Mrs Truong is smiling like she gets the irony. "Well, Carrie, I don't think it's nuts. It makes sense and I have a story for you that you might like to hear."

She has that thinking look of hers on again. "Thank you. I'd like to hear your story."

"When we were in Villawood something similar happened to Mai-Ling. The children were bored a lot of the time, as I have told you before, and this often led to mischief. She was friends with this group of girls who were not good for her but she would not listen to me."

She is pausing like she is waiting for me to respond in some way. I just nod and she continues.

"One day, one of these girls asked her to steal something for her. It was something small but meant to prove that Mai-Ling was part of the gang. She did as she was asked but got caught. Then when the security guard asked why she did it she said she had been dared. The other girl then got into trouble as well and from then on the whole gang made Mai-Ling's life very difficult. She learned very quickly not to speak out about anyone or anything – and not to get caught in the first place."

I sort of give Mrs Truong a knowing smile, "I've got to agree with you there, she certainly had that one wrapped up."

She smiles back at me and continues.

"I worried my daughter would be led astray but luckily we left soon after that. Mai-Ling would have respected you for not telling the security guard that she had also taken a pair of sunglasses."

"We kind of had an understanding of each other after that. You know, she still had them, she just hid them better than me."

Mrs Truong suddenly looks old and sad again as she shakes her head and stares hard at the ground. Jesus, I shouldn't have said that. "Mrs Truong, it wasn't like she took things . . ."

Mrs Truong is not listening, she is thinking about something else. "Carrie, that is why she never told you the truth about her scholarship."

"Because of the sunglasses?"

"No. Because she knew what would happen if she did."

A cold shiver washes down my spine as I remember the look on Pham's face earlier tonight as he glared at me from his car.

CHAPTER 10

Mrs Truong is starting to shiver. She is trying to disguise it by clasping her hands tightly in her lap. I can see by the way she is biting her lip that she is near breaking point. I reach over and put my hand on hers. I wonder whether I should hug her or something, like the way she hugged me. I can't though, I feel too awkward.

Instead, I lean over and pull her head onto my shoulder. "It will be okay, Mrs Truong. I promise." She is quivering all over now and I can feel her tears soaking through my top onto my shoulder. "Shall I get you some water or something?"

"I need to see Mai-Ling. I just need to see my daughter. I need to tell her . . . I need to tell her I love her," she whispers.

I'm choking on my words and the tears are streaming down my face. "I will go and find someone; I will make them listen to me. Wait here, okay? I'll be right back."

All the faces on the front desk are new but I won't be fobbed off again so I rehearse what I'm going to say if I get another *no*. I choose the nurse who looks the friendliest and stride up like she is just waiting for the chance to help me.

"Hi, I brought my friend Mai-Ling in here a few hours ago and I need to . . ." She is looking back at me like she has no idea who I am talking about. "Mai-Ling, the Vietnamese girl, she was really sick and . . ."

"Oh, yes I know who you mean . . . we were wondering if anyone had been told she was here."

"What do you mean? Her mum and I have been sitting here for hours! We've been asking to see her for ages."

The woman looks genuinely surprised. "I'm sorry. I've only been here for the last hour or so. The last shift didn't mention anything."

"Christ! Her mum is beside herself with worry. No-one will tell us anything and no-one will let us see her and . . ." I am almost screaming at her as I point out Mrs Truong so that she can see just how upset she is.

"I'll find out what is happening for you."

Shit, I was all prepared for a fight and I can't believe what she just said. I nod at Mrs Truong and her eyes brighten as her face loses some of its tension. Suddenly I feel like I can sort this out, you know, really can fix it after all.

The nurse returns in a few minutes with a doctor. Not the doctor I spoke to before, someone new.

"Hi, I'm Dr Lindal. Sorry about the mix up. No-one told us you were here." He is holding out his hand and I go to shake it but as I clutch it I realise he is pointing to the chairs behind us.

"Please, sit down."

My face burns and my stomach sinks with embarrassment. "Yeah, thanks."

He smiles back like it does not matter to him that I am a total idiot. "Does Mai-Ling's mother speak English?"

"Yes."

"Good. I would like to talk to you both."

We sit down and I introduce Mrs Truong to the doctor. He looks at her with real compassion, unlike that other jerk.

"Mrs Truong, your daughter is stable at the moment but has not regained consciousness. I know this is very distressing for you but I want you to know we are doing everything we can. I am sorry to have to be the one telling you this but I think it is important that you understand that there is a strong possibility that she may not regain consciousness."

I feel like I've been punched in the guts. I blurt out, "Do you mean she might die?"

The doctor nods long before he speaks. "It is possible."

I watch Mrs Truong for a reaction but she just stares at the doctor with a neutral expression on her face. It is like she has heard the words but they have not filtered through to her brain yet.

I hold her hand and look directly at the doctor. "Can we see her? Just for a minute even?"

He nods. Thank God!

"Not for long, but yes, you can both come in and see her."

Mrs Truong is crying as I help her up. I am so grateful that someone is actually listening to us that I want to cry too but I won't let myself. I want to be strong for Mrs Truong, to be the one who's there for her this time. I smile back at the doctor instead. "Thanks so much."

He gives me an appreciative look. "The nurse will take you through."

I take Mrs Truong's forearm and guide her past the plastic doors, the same doors that until now have been such a barrier. We walk down the corridor and turn into Mai-Ling's room.

The minute I see Mai-Ling lying there on the bed I am taken aback. It is Mai-Ling alright but no-one has prepared us for how terrible she looks right now. I can hardly recognise her. Her skin is grey and her hair is matted and limp. She looks vacant, with her mouth open and drooping to one side. Jesus, there is even a string of drool hanging from the corner and pooling on her pillow. Mrs Truong is staring at her too with disbelief.

I gently take her arm and walk her over to the bed. I'm scared shitless but unless I do something we'd both be standing in the doorway like fools for ever. I am torn between staying with Mrs Truong and giving her some space. I choose to step back.

She just stands there for a few minutes watching Mai-Ling breathe. I am helpless, totally helpless. "Mrs Truong?"

She doesn't answer me. "Are you okay, Mrs Truong?"

Christ, she is crying. Not the quiet tears of before, this is loud heartfelt sobbing. She is saying something over and over in Vietnamese as she wraps herself over Mai-Ling and cradles her head. Then, in a desperate whisper she says something in English.

"I am sorry, I am so sorry, please don't die, please don't die my beautiful girl. I love you Maia . . . I love you . . ."

I watch Mrs Truong's despair. I am frozen, powerless. How can I tell her what really happened tonight? How?

The nurse has come in now and is taking Mrs Truong out of the room. I follow. I cannot look back at Mai-Ling. Seeing her like that, it is all too real and I just can't . . .

Back in our same seats, our island, neither of us speaks. I am too frightened to break the ice in case Mrs Truong goes into a total meltdown. I can't handle this anymore. I wish I'd not seen Mai-Ling. Not seen her like that.

I want to retreat to my toilet cubicle again but Mrs Truong grabs my arm as I start to get up. She is holding it tighter than ever.

"I was looking forward to the day when Mai-Ling got married. To see her as a bride."

"And you will, Mrs Truong. She will get married one day and you will be there."

"She is dying Carrie."

Her words sting so hard that I have to swallow the puke that has erupted in my throat. "No, she's going to be okay. I just know it. Don't give up. She won't die!"

"Do you have a boyfriend, Carrie?"

"A boyfriend?"

"Yes, I never asked you that before. I asked about Mai-Ling having a boyfriend but I never asked you."

I look into her eyes to see if she is still focusing. It is like she has lost the plot or something. Why would she care if I had a boyfriend, you know, at a time like this?

"I need you to keep telling me your story. Please, Carrie, this pain in my heart is so great. I need to take my mind to happier times."

I get it. Christ I get it. I feel the pain she is talking about too and I suddenly feel a real connection with her. "Okay."

I decide to tell her about something that I have not told anyone but Mai-Ling before. I take a deep breath and restart my story like this.

I had a boyfriend before Mai-Ling and I were really good friends. We were together for about a year but he dumped me for this other chick. I was pretty heartbroken but I thought I got over it pretty quickly.

Anyway, one night, when I was out in the city with Mai-Ling, I got this text from him, "hey sxc i no now i made a mistake lettin u go. Any chance i cud make it up 2 u?"

I was really excited but I didn't tell Mai-Ling. I replied "U can try 2 make it up 2 me". Then he messaged that he was at a club in the city and I should hook up with him there, just us.

It was really slack but I told Mai-Ling some bullshit about having to get home and then raced straight over there.

We had a great night and I ended up going back to his place for. . . well anyway I was back being his girlfriend and I was really happy.

The stupid thing was, I really hated the type of girls who dumped their girlfriends the minute a guy was on the scene. I didn't mean it to be that way but I couldn't help myself. I would put everyone off from making plans just in case he wanted to see me that night, or worse still I'd dump my girlfriends if he called last minute.

I knew Mai-Ling was getting the shits because in the end she stopped making plans with me and for a while I didn't see much of her. You know, I was so involved in Steve's world that my girlfriends didn't matter anymore.

Then one night at a party, Steve asked me to come up to one of the bedrooms. I was pretty drunk and it seemed like a great idea at the time.

When I got up there though, one of his friends was there smoking a joint. I thought

Steve would ask him to leave. Instead he sat down on the floor with him and his friend passed me the joint. I was pretty out of it already and joined them on the floor for a smoke.

After about five minutes his friend leaned over and started to kiss me. He moved his hand under my top and well, you know started getting . . . anyway. I was expecting Steve to punch him or something but to my surprise he didn't. I looked up at him and he was taking photos with his phone camera.

I couldn't believe it. I could hardly think straight let alone walk straight, and when I tried to push his mate off me he pinned me down and started ripping off my clothes. I was screaming "No, No! Make him stop, Steve!" but he ignored me. I couldn't make him stop and with the music blaring, no-one else could hear me.

He had sex with me and so did Steve and I was crying and everything but they didn't care, they just kept going. They kept taking photos and everything all the way through like I was some porno star or something.

As I tell my story I can feel my chest tighten and I am finding it hard to breathe. Shit! I am feeling the same panic I felt back then. I am shaking, and the room feels like it is ten times smaller. Sweat is trickling down into my eyes as I gasp for air.

Mrs Truong's hand is on my shoulder. "Carrie. . . are you alright Carrie?"

My voice has gone really crackly. I want to run outside and puke but my head has become so confused that I cannot move. I suck in air and smile back at her, "I'm okay. Thanks."

"You don't have to continue . . ."

"No, truly, I can go on." I take a deep breath and focus. It has suddenly become important to me that I tell it to the end so I push my anxiety to the side and continue with my story.

When they were finished, Steve and his mate just left me there in the room. It took ages to get dressed and to go back out to the party. I knew they had all these photos on Steve's phone and they were probably showing everyone. I was totally shamed and alone. I didn't know what to do. I had dissed all my girlfriends for the past month, even Mai-Ling, and didn't feel I could call any of them.

I wandered around outside in the street for ages. It was kind of surreal. I knew I had been raped but I thought that maybe it didn't count because I was with my boyfriend or something. Like, who would believe me anyway? It wasn't like I was an angel in the first place.

Eventually I got a cab and called Mai-Ling. I didn't know what else to do. And despite everything she came straight over to help me. She didn't once say any of the things she could have said, she was just there for me. She was a true friend that night and I'll never forget it. She let me prattle on and cry and she just listened, never once judging me or anything.

I stop talking because I am crying again, but this time I am not crying for me. I am crying because I know how much I have let Mai-Ling down tonight.

Mrs Truong is looking at me with such compassion in her eyes. She is not judging me at all even though I deserve to be judged. I know I don't deserve her kindness but I feel a sort of bond with her right now and I need to talk to her. I really need to tell her how I felt that night so I continue to spill my words, in between my sobs.

I had never felt so vulnerable in my life before. I had put myself in a situation where I couldn't even look after myself because I was so drunk. I trusted Steve, I thought I was okay because he was there but I realised later that if my girlfriends had been around, even if they had all been off with other guys, if we had all been looking out for each other at the party then I probably would have been okay.

I gaze up at Mrs Truong who is looking silently at me, "Do you know what I mean?"

Mrs Truong nods and squeezes my hand but I know what she is thinking. Where was I tonight? Why wasn't I looking out for Mai-Ling?

CHAPTER 11

We sit and stare at the plastic doors. Shit! I wish I'd never told Mrs Truong that last part of my story. In fact it really pisses me off that I am the only one having to share all my stuff while Mrs Truong gets to sit there and judge me. You know, it is not like it is all my fault. Mrs Truong is to blame for some of it, she just doesn't realise it, that's all. Suddenly, her eyes are locked on mine. I am convinced she can read my mind!

"Carrie, it just doesn't make sense. It is like one day Mai-Ling became a totally different person. I can't explain it but I know something happened, I just don't know what."

I know what. I know exactly what. I could come straight out and tell her but that would be a huge slap in the face for her. You see, I was there the day Mai-Ling lost respect for her mum. She was there too but she wasn't aware of it. That's why she is partly to blame for all of this. And here I am spilling my guts about everything and Mrs Truong . . . oh fuck it, it's time to deliver a dose of reality.

"Mrs Truong, I think I know what happened . . ."

She is looking at the ground and nodding slowly. "It's something I did, isn't it?"

"Kind of."

"I have thought a lot about what it could have been. If you can tell me . . ."

"I might be wrong, though, so don't take . . ."

"It is better to know. Even if it is bad, so please I would like you to tell me."

"Okay, if you're sure."

I've gone too far to pull out now so here goes.

Mai-Ling was pretty obsessed with study. She was dead keen to get into medicine next year at uni. Anyway, after the exam trials she didn't take a break like the rest of us. We all took a couple of weeks off to party and relax but not Mai-Ling. She just kept the pace up and I hardly saw her because she was always at the library with her nose in some humungous book.

Then, one day, she was at the train station early, and when I asked her why she wasn't at the library she said that she had a headache and was going straight home instead. I said that I'd come with her so we could hang out for the afternoon.

When we got back to the house, we let ourselves in, not expecting anyone else to be home. But as soon as we opened the door, I could tell that something was wrong. Mai-Ling went really quiet and just stared at a bunch of keys sitting on the coffee table. I asked her if her mum had forgotten them. She didn't answer but the expression on her face told me to shut up. I could hear noises from the bedroom and I tried to suggest that we could go back to my place instead of staying there but she like totally ignored me. She just stood there looking down the hallway.

I take a breath before going on because I am looking at Mrs Truong and I'm guessing that she knows what is coming. Her face has gone kind of pale and she won't look me in the eye. I should stop now but I don't want to. I am being a total bitch but she needs to take some responsibility for all this shit as well. I want her to know that this thing tonight is not all my fault so I pretend I haven't noticed that she is upset, and go on.

I thought Mai-Ling would come after me but she didn't. Instead she started walking down the hallway, straight for the bedroom. I ran after her telling her to come back. She spun around and glared, you know, with this back-off kind of look. So I just shut up and followed her.

At the end of the hallway I could see that the bedroom door was partially open and I could see Pham and her mum together . . . well not exactly see . . . shit, you know, but it was pretty obvious what was going on . . .

I am pausing again because I know I have gone too far. The colour has returned to Mrs Truong's face. It is not embarrassment but shame I see. Come on, I'm thinking. Everyone has sex. It's not like it is that big a deal.

I put my hand on her arm momentarily. "I know you feel embarrassed Mrs Truong but we didn't see anything graphic if that makes you feel any better."

As she shakes her head, the tears on her cheek catch the light. Suddenly I don't feel like saying any more but I've pushed it too far and there is no going back.

"Carrie, I didn't know Mai-Ling knew. I would have talked to her about it.

She never . . ."

"She couldn't talk about it. She couldn't even talk to me about it. I don't know why she took it so hard. I didn't think it was such a big deal myself."

There I go, letting her off the hook. You watch, by the end of tonight everything will be my fault and I bet she won't be there making excuses for me!

"Do you want me to tell you the rest?" She is wiping her eyes and trying to smile. It's a pretty poor attempt but I smile back and keep going.

Mai-Ling just stood there for a few minutes then turned and left. I took off after her and by the time I had caught up she had gone from being really upset to being really angry. I had never seen her like that before. She was like, kicking this fence, and swearing and stuff.

I tried to calm her down but it only made things worse. I told her that her mum had been on her own for a long time and it was good that she had someone. Well, she went into a spin with this and started screaming at me that I was a fuckwit if I believed that, and I had no idea what I was talking about. She went on to say that I knew jack about anything in her life. Then she said that her mother had disgraced her father by doing this. I probably shouldn't have said anything but I wanted to make her wake up to herself, she wasn't making any sense. I screamed back at her that her father was dead and had nothing to do with it.

That's when she stopped shouting and gave me this real death stare. Her eyes looked like they were on fire. I was about to start shouting at her to grow up or something, when she started crying. Real heartfelt crying. She sort of folded into a heap on the footpath and sobbed into her hands.

After that she wouldn't let me even mention what had happened. It was like it was this forbidden subject and if I asked her about it she would look at me like she didn't know what I was talking about.

She stopped studying after that too and became this real party girl. At first, I figured she was just rebelling against all the pressure she had been under with studying for exams and stuff. I actually sort of encouraged it because it meant we could start hanging out again.

It was just like before, when we spent the summer holidays at my house. I would help her with the office cleaning and then we'd be out till all hours clubbing and having fun. I knew we would have to hit the books again sooner or later. I thought Mai-Ling was just letting her hair down for a bit.

But by about August I started to realise that she had changed more than I thought. I was back on the straight and narrow, getting stuck into my school work, but not Mai-Ling. She was still out nearly every night, often on her own, drinking and picking up guys. It was then that I realised that something was terribly wrong.

I tried to talk to her about it but she wouldn't listen to me. Then one night when we were out she got so drunk that on the way home she was sitting on the footpath, spewing into the gutter and I was helping hold her head up. I told her that she was getting out of control and that people were starting to say things, you know, like she was a slut and stuff. I said it to try to shock her into listening to me, but it didn't work. She just kind of laughed and said, "Like mother, like daughter".

That's when the penny dropped. I couldn't believe she was still going on about her mum and Pham. I told her to get herself a bottle of harden-the-fuck-up and get over it. I left her there still spewing in the gutter and went home.

The next day she rang me and said she was sorry. She kind of settled down a bit after that too, you know, stopped being so wild. I actually thought I'd gotten through to her.

Until tonight that is . . .

Fuck, those voices in my head are at me again.

I have finished. I don't want to tell any more and I am hoping Mrs Truong doesn't push it. She has her thinking face on again so I know she is about to say something.

"It wasn't like that with me and Pham. It was more about friendship than sex."

Christ, she expects me to believe that?

"I think Mai-Ling was missing her dad. It wasn't really about you, that whole thing just triggered something in her, that's all," I said, trying to soften the mood.

"Her father meant a lot to her. She lost him such a tragic way."

I am taken aback by this because even though I knew Mai-Ling's father died on the way out here I had never thought to ask how it happened. I guess I assumed he just died in his sleep or something.

"To be honest Mai-Ling never really talked about *how* her dad actually died."

"She never told you that we were attacked by pirates?"

"Jesus, no!"

"I see. I thought it was only me who she wouldn't discuss this with, but now I realise she couldn't talk about it at all. Well then, I'll tell you what happened."

As Mrs Truong starts talking about her past, a sadness washes over her face and her voice cracks slightly.

"They came in the night while most of us slept. We were not prepared. We had nothing to defend ourselves with. They had guns and knives. They were ruthless men. You could see it in their eyes as they ransacked our tiny boat. Cruel people with no respect for life."

"Oh my God! It must have been really frightening."

"We had all heard stories about men like this. How they raped and murdered whole boatloads of people."

"So, what did you do?"

"Mai-Ling's father tried to stop them. He had nothing but a bamboo stick. They shot him in the legs and he fell to the deck. Everyone else cowered in a huddle. I tried to hide Mai-Ling behind me. I was afraid of what might happen if they saw her. I wanted to go to my husband, to help him. He was screaming in pain and there was blood everywhere but I was too afraid to move."

I am feeling sick to my stomach. "What did the pirates do?"

"They took everything they could get their hands on and left. They took all our food and most of our water. We were only lucky they didn't find the small amount of water we had hidden."

"And Mai-Ling's dad?"

"We stopped the bleeding as best we could. I tore the hem of my dress for bandages but we couldn't get the bullets out. He would have lived if we had had proper medicine but we had nothing. Infection set in and ate away half his leg before it took his life almost a week later. He died in terrible pain."

"Oh Jesus."

"Conditions on the boat were unbearable with only a small amount of water and no food. People started going mad in the searing heat. We had no way of burying my husband's body and I was afraid of what might happen if it was left on the boat. So during the night I threw it overboard. In the morning, I told Mai-Ling that the spirits had taken him to a better place. She was only twelve."

My mind is racing over what Mrs Truong is saying. Mai-Ling never talked about any of this. Sure she told me her father died on the way over here but I never thought . . . Christ!

"I'm so sorry, Mrs Truong. It must have been . . ." I cannot even think of a word to describe it. "How did you survive? I mean with no food for all that time?"

"Two days later we were picked up by a Navy ship. We had rationed the little bit of water we had left but we had all but given up. If the ship had not stopped we would have all died. God was looking after us that day."

"That's amazing. You're amazing." This just poured out of my mouth but I really mean it. Christ, I have lived like a princess compared to this and I have never once thanked anyone, let alone God. It makes me seriously wonder what sort of a person I really am. I hate to think how I would have survived if our lives had been reversed.

Mrs Truong is smiling. "Thank you."

Her thank you is so genuine that it makes me feel like such a fraud. I am struck by the urgent need to tell her the truth about me.

I need to tell her what happened tonight. I need to tell her right now.

"I don't deserve your thank you, Mrs Truong. I really don't. I wanted to tell you the story about Mai-Ling finding you in bed with Pham so that this whole thing didn't look like it was all my fault. I wanted you to feel like it was your fault too, but it isn't. None of this is. Mai-Ling is here tonight because of something I have done. Something I am really sorry about but I . . ."

"No Carrie, you cannot blame yourself. Mai-Ling has a wonderful friend in you. She made a mistake tonight. She took something, a drug of some kind, but it isn't your fault."

"But I . . ."

"This is *my* fault. If I had been more honest with Mai-Ling. If I had told her about my relationship with Pham then perhaps she could have confided in me and perhaps things would have been different."

I open my mouth. I need to confess the terrible thing I did tonight. I need to say it right now, before I lose courage. But the words catch in my throat. Mai-Ling's words, *"like mother, like daughter"* are echoing in my head as I replay Mrs Truong's last statement. Shit, Mai-Ling was trying to tell me way back then what Pham was doing to her. Christ! I could have done something, helped her. I was just too fucking stupid to get it.

CHAPTER 12

"Mrs Truong?"

"Yes, Carrie?"

"I really screwed up tonight."

"You did what you could for Mai-Ling. I know you did."

"I should have realised that things were out of control months ago. I was so stupid. I thought we were just having fun. Being wild and all that. I didn't think about what could happen."

"I have made many mistakes in my life too, Carrie. We all do. And you are young."

"No, Mrs Truong, I did something really terrible tonight and I have to tell you. Please, just let me say it. I know you will hate me for it and I'm really sorry about that because, well, over these last few hours I've started to think if things had been different. I mean I just wish I'd got to know you better before, that's all. I think we could have been friends."

"We are friends. You have given me a true gift tonight. You don't realise how much your story has meant to me. Whatever you have to say won't change that."

"I know it will but thank you."

I want to cry but if I give in to myself I will never be able to say what I need to say. My stomach is churning and I want to puke. Jesus, this is the hardest thing I have ever done. I take a deep breath and swallow the lump in my throat.

I need to start way back, before tonight, so that Mrs Truong kind of understands why things got so crazy. I say this to myself but I know it won't make any difference. I am condemned and there is no way out of it. Still, this is how I choose to tell it, the story of the moment when my life changed forever and Mrs Truong just has to know it too.

Mai-Ling and I did end up swotting for the HSC exams but we didn't work as hard as we should have. That's because we spent more time going out than a lot of the other kids. I kind of had myself convinced that it made us study harder if we had a bit of pressure.

Once the exams were over, however, we both really cut loose. It was like I had my fabulous best friend back again. Mai-Ling was just like I was, and when we went out we partied hard. We were inseparable and it was fantastic.

Things were perfect, that is until about a month ago. I noticed that Mai-Ling was changing and little things started happening. I don't mean she was getting really studious again. It was like she was going beyond fun and getting really moody and stuff.

Some nights she wouldn't answer her phone or even return my text messages. When I mentioned it to her, she kind of threw the shutters down on me. I thought she must have had a boyfriend or something that she didn't want to tell me about. It was so stupid really because I hadn't noticed that anything had happened to bring this on. Not like before with – well, you know.

Then, one day, I was like phoning her every half hour and she wouldn't pick up. I was certain she was at home and that really pissed me off, so I drove over to have it out with her.

As I pulled up, I saw Pham getting into his car and driving away. I didn't think a whole lot about it at the time because I figured that her mum must have been home.

Anyway, I was about to drive off as well when I saw Mai-Ling come outside. She had something in her hands which she was putting into the bin.

I jumped out of my car and surprised her. She tried to cover up what she was throwing out but I'd already seen it. It was a pair of underpants. Hers, I imagine. I didn't say anything about it at the time. I thought she must have had her – well, you know . . .

The odd bit was that she was acting really normally. You know, since I'd seen that Pham had been there, I thought she must have finally sorted the whole thing out with her mum. But when I broached the subject, she denied Pham had been there at all.

Mrs Truong is looking at me, like she is waiting for me to say something bad about her again, but this is not about her – it's about me.

Anyway, that was a few weeks ago now. Things seemed to go back to normal after that but there was this unspoken agreement that I didn't ask her any questions about things at home, and she wouldn't act so moody.

And that's how it was until tonight, when we were at this party in Newtown. We had been in the city earlier and met these guys who asked us to come along with them. They were really cute and it seemed like a great idea.

It was a great night – to start with. Mai-Ling and I were like, talking to everyone and really having fun. Mai-Ling hooked up with one of the guys who had invited us there and they were getting on well until she went off to take a phone call. After that she was acting really weird. I had hooked up with this other guy and we were kissing and stuff in the lounge when Mai-Ling came over and started to hit on him. I couldn't believe it; she had never done that to me before. She was really going for it, too. You know – more than just flirting.

I was so pissed off with her that I dragged her out to the kitchen to tell her to wake up to *herself, and back off. She was pretty drunk though, and by the time I got her outside she was like, apologising for everything, and I sort of didn't feel like I could go off at her anymore. I got her a drink of water and made her sit and talk to me for a bit to try to sober her up. That's when I saw Pham through the kitchen window. He was parked outside the house and just leaning on his car like he was waiting for someone.*

I couldn't believe he was there. As I turned to tell Mai-Ling, I could see on her face that she already knew. Things started adding up; you know, all the stuff that had happened before and suddenly I realised what was going on.

I just stared at her and shook my head and she knew that I knew. Huge tears welled up in her eyes and started rolling down her face, but all I could say to her was, "You can't be serious? Pham is your boyfriend?"

She was sobbing and almost choking on her tears, but I kept going, "That's why you were so pissed off that day when you saw him with your mum. Mai-Ling, he's like fifty something. What's the matter with you?"

She kept shaking her head and saying, "No, he's not my boyfriend!"

But I kept on. "How did he know we were here, then? Come on, Mai-Ling. I'm not fucking stupid! What I don't get is why him? He's such a creep and you can do so much better."

That's when she started screaming back at me, "He's not my boyfriend, he's my mother's boyfriend. He's having sex with me but he's her boyfriend."

"He's what?"

"He's making me have sex with him," Mai-Ling screamed back at me. "He says that if I don't he'll make big trouble for my mum. He says he will dob her in to the tax and immigration, and worse. He's dangerous Carrie, really dangerous, and if I don't do what he says, then I don't know what he'll do."

"What are you talking about?"

"He'll do something terrible to us. You don't mess with Pham, Carrie. You do what he wants."

I could see that she was terrified. I was so angry that the bastard thought he could get away with doing that to Mai-Ling. I wanted to help her, to make him pay for what he was doing. So I ran outside and started yelling stuff at him, telling him to get the fuck away from Mai-Ling. I called him a paedophile and everything, but he didn't even acknowledge me. It was like I was nothing.

He looked straight past me and started calling out to Mai-Ling in Vietnamese. He must have been telling her to get in the car. She came to the door and I was screaming at her to go back inside. Then Pham started slowly walking towards us. He was so intimidating. He was holding something which kind of flashed in the moonlight and I thought it was a knife. I was so scared that I picked up some bottles from the ground and

just threw them at him, one after another. I
hit him, too, right in the chest.

Mai-Ling was going crazy. She was crying
and shouting at me to stop but I kept going. I
had to, because by now he was coming right
for me. I knew I was in for it and I'd run out
of bottles. I needed to distract him so I could
make a run for it back inside, so I started
hurling rocks at his precious car instead. He
was threatening me with all kinds of stuff,
and people from the party started coming
outside. He narrowed his eyes and stared at
me and I knew he really wanted to hurt me. By
that time, there was quite a crowd watching
us. He just got back into his car and took off.

After that, Mai-Ling was a real mess.
She couldn't stop crying. She kept saying I'd
fucked everything up and that Pham would
make everyone pay for what I'd done. I
thought she was overreacting. I had no idea
who I was dealing with. All I knew was that
I had to make everything alright again, so I
did something to try to fix it. I just wanted to
try to help Mai-Ling calm down so she could
hear reason.

I am shaking all over now. Mrs Truong is looking at me so intently her eyes are burning into mine like a laser. As she waits for me to finish my story, hot tears begin cascading down my cheeks.

"Mrs Truong, *I* gave it to her. I gave her the ecstasy tablet!"

Our eyes lock as I wait for a reaction. Mrs Truong is just staring blankly back at me like she hasn't heard a word I said. "I told her to break it in half. To share it with me but she was too upset to hear me properly. Before I could stop her, she just swallowed the whole thing. I thought it would help calm her down. I thought I was helping her . . ." I am trying to speak coherently but my words are coming out broken and torn. I desperately need Mrs Truong to say something but she is just staring at me.

"I'm so sorry, Mrs Truong. I didn't mean things to end up like this, I was just trying to . . ." She is just looking at me blankly and I can't stop babbling on. "But if she dies tonight, oh God, if she dies I'll hate myself forever. I'm so sorry. I know you must hate me now. Christ I hate me."

Mrs Truong has taken my hand and breaks her silence. "Carrie, I don't hate you."

I am trembling so much I can hardly speak. "But you should."

"It's myself I hate for turning a blind eye to what Pham was doing. For not being a good mother to my daughter. For not protecting Mai-Ling. These things are not your fault, Carrie. They're mine. All mine."

"No Mrs Truong, it's mine too."

"No, it's true. I allowed my debt to Pham to become so great that my own daughter was used as a payback. He has always taken whatever he wanted from us. He owns us, and now that I have sacrificed everything to him, I only have my Mai-Ling left. I only have my beautiful daughter, and now she is dying."

Mrs Truong breaks into sobs and I put my arms around her. We are both crying now, holding tightly to each other.

As I let the entrails of my dirty secret fall to the ground I feel the hopelessness of the situation strangle me like a python crushing a mouse. It is a no win whichever way it goes. Our lives are fucked from this point onwards and there is no turning back. If Mai-Ling dies, I will never forgive myself but if Mai-Ling lives it will be Mrs Truong who will never be forgiven.

CHAPTER 13

As I rest my head on Mrs Truong's shoulder, I can see the beginnings of daylight creep through the window behind us. With the night's grey shadows slowly dissolving in front of me, I feel like I have stepped into a parallel universe – some kind of time warp perhaps. It's like there were a million possibilities for last night and Mai-Ling and I just stepped through the wrong fucking door. Christ, this whole thing is unreal.

Right about now we should be walking down the street, shoes in hand, looking for a cab to go home. We should be talking about the night like it was just a stepping stone to the next. You know, making plans about which guys we would see again and what clubs we would check out next.

I always thought the worst thing that could happen to me would be something like catching herpes or getting pregnant. Fuck, I never imagined anything like this.

We have been waiting for hours for someone to tell us what the hell is going on with Mai-Ling. It is like we are lost at sea, marooned on our tiny island and hoping like crazy that someone will burst through those plastic doors and rescue us.

I am shit scared to even let myself think, because I can only imagine the worst. It's like I'm fighting ghosts and it's freaking me out. For fuck's sake, even the voices in my head have gone dead quiet and an eerie silence has fallen in their place.

There are no words of support from anyone. There are no promises and worse still there are no lies. Just a spoilt teenager and a middle-aged Vietnamese woman left to comfort each other and wait for God only knows what.

I have been telling Mrs Truong my story because she needs something to hang onto, but we both know it's a waste of time. We are both reading between the lines. We have both picked up on the subplot underpinning the narrative, which is playing out like a classic whodunit. There are clues which allude to a possible conclusion but right up to the last page we will still be guessing. All the way along we will tell ourselves that surely this cannot be it, that there must be something missing. But as we read the last line we will have to accept that there is no more. That it all finishes so abruptly. No explanations, no tying up of loose ends, just 'The End' full-stop.

I spiral into fear again and clutch Mrs Truong even more tightly. She responds by hugging me back and I try to hide my tears but they are drenching her blouse. I am tired and emotionally drained and I'd give anything to be somewhere else right now.

The dawn waiting room is finally quiet. The nurses at the triage station float in and out calling the occasional name but not ours. We have both come to expect this now and do not even lift our heads up.

But as I say this, as if to make a liar out of me, a young-looking doctor bursts through the plastic doors and heads straight for us. The nurse following him is pointing at Mrs Truong and as if on cue we both jump up. Mrs Truong's hand tightens over mine as we brace ourselves.

"This is the mother, Mrs Truong," the nurse says.

My stomach plummets to the floor. Their faces tell me that this is not good news and my words hardly manage to claw their way out of my mouth: "Is it Mai-Ling? What's happening?" I search for an answer in their expressions but they're giving nothing away.

The doctor looks directly at Mrs Truong, "You are Mai-Ling's mother?"

As she struggles to reply I step in. "Yes, she is. What's happening? Where is the doctor we spoke to last time?"

"Do you speak English Mrs Truong?" The doctor is speaking so slowly it is embarrassing. What is his problem? Does he think we are both morons or something?

Mrs Truong is nodding and the doctor gives the nurse a sideways glance like he is now the one searching for words.

I cannot hold on any longer. "Is she dead? For fuck's sake, just tell us. Is she dead?"

The doctor is now looking straight at me. His lips quiver slightly like he is about to answer but he remains silent. A chill freezes me to the spot and sweat is running off my face like I'm caught in the rain. All I can manage is a hoarse whisper, "Is she?"

His answer is directed to Mrs Truong, "I'm sorry, we can't do anything more for your daughter. You should come through now and see her."

"No! You have to be able to do something!" I beg but he just shakes his head. Mrs Truong is looking at me quizzically like I need to translate the doctor's words but I cannot bring myself to say more. Instead, I take her arm as we follow the doctor back through the plastic doors.

I let Mrs Truong go to Mai-Ling first and hang back in the door. Not that I'm being noble or kind or shit like that; I am being a fucking coward pretending to do the right thing.

At first I think Mai-Ling is still unconscious but as Mrs Truong leans over and kisses her cheek, her eyes open. My heart skips a beat and for a moment a wave of relief takes my breath away. It is like the nightmare has dissolved in this instant, I'm awake and everything is alright. Then the moment disappears just as quickly as it came. As I look more closely at Mai-Ling I realise that her eyes are hardly focused. She is barely aware we are in the room.

Mrs Truong is holding her, sobbing and rocking her back and forth, mumbling in Vietnamese. Every now and then she says something in English and I can fill in the rest as if I understood every word. She keeps telling Mai-Ling how much she loves her, that she is her beautiful little girl and that she will get well. I can feel Mrs Truong's desperation as if it were my own.

We have shared so much tonight, not just our stories but our dark secrets too. As I stand in the doorway watching her brush Mai-Ling's face with the back of her hand, begging for some sign of recognition, my heart breaks in two. She has sacrificed everything for her daughter. She has lost her husband, her freedom and even her dignity to give Mai-Ling a better life. And now, in one careless moment, one total act of stupidity, everything she has done has turned to shit. I can only stand and watch helplessly. I want to tell Mai-Ling so many things. What an idiot I was to give her the ecstasy, not to see what was happening to her and how, if she would just get through this, I would make it up to her.

I want to run to the bed and shake her, make her sit up and say that she is okay, that all this was just a bad dream. But I cannot move any further into the room. I am immobilised in the doorway.

As I choke back tears, a voice startles me from behind. Jesus Christ, it can't be . . . as I spin around, I recoil as I come face to face with Pham. His cold stare sends shivers down my spine and I stumble backwards into the room.

I can hear the relief in Mrs Truong's voice as she calls his name and bursts into tears. I cannot believe her reaction. She knows what he has done to Mai-Ling. She knows better than anyone what a total creep he is. I stare in disbelief but she is under his spell. Leaving Mai-Ling's side, she embraces him and cries into his designer shirt.

Christ, I cannot let him near Mai-Ling. He has no right to be here, no right to be anywhere *near* her. As my eyes meet his, a mixture of hate and fear floods my mind. There is no-one around to protect us, the doctor is nowhere to be seen and Pham's menacing presence blocks my exit. I know too much about him to muster the bravado I had earlier in the night. I turn to Mrs Truong but her eyes are pleading with a don't-make-waves look. I am in a no-win situation, I am scared shitless of this man but I cannot let Mai-Ling down again. My mind flashes back to Mrs Truong's story about the pirates and I can only imagine how scared she must have been. I take a deep breath and my words flow unemotionally and clearly, "You have no right to be here. Get out!"

He ignores me and starts speaking to Mrs Truong in Vietnamese. She acts like he is her knight in shining armour. I am totally fucking gobsmacked.

As Mrs Truong gabbles, Pham keeps looking over at me. She is talking about me but I have no idea what she is saying. I can tell by the tone of his voice that he is interrogating her. He is holding her as she sobs her answers to his relentless questions. And all the while I can feel his glare burning into me like a magnifying glass held to the light.

Turning away, I look back at Mai-Ling. I think I see her hand move. As I reach over to her, her eyes lock with mine. She tries to say something but her mouth cannot form the words. She is cold, really cold and I start screaming out for the doctor. Mai-Ling is shaking all over and she is gagging on something. "Get the doctor! Get the doctor!"

People come running in. A nurse tries to elbow me aside but I won't leave Mai-Ling. "What's happening? Mai-Ling! Mai-Ling!"

The doctor turns to me, "Get her mother."

I can't think, everything is happening so fast. Pham is holding on to Mrs Truong, who is trying to pull away.

I am screaming at him. "Let her go!"

Pham mutters something in Vietnamese and releases Mrs Truong. She pushes past the nurses and throws herself on Mai-

Ling's bed. She is wailing Mai-Ling's name over and over as everyone in the room goes deathly quiet. I glance from face to face and every look is the same. "No! No! Do something!" I am hysterical. Mai-Ling is lying with her eyes wide open, staring at us but there is no light in them. "Help her. Someone help her!"

The doctor gently closes her eyes and shakes his head. "I'm sorry."

Mrs Truong stares at me. She looks so lost, so bewildered. I am shaking, my screaming now a whimper. I am too numb to say or do more.

The doctor is moving me out of the room but I am resisting.

His voice is quiet but firm. "I think it is best to give Mai-Ling's parents some time alone."

"But that's not . . ." As the words spill out of my mouth, Pham glowers and his bony index finger rises and points accusingly at me.

"I know what you have done. You have killed our Mai-Ling."

I can feel the blood drain from my face as a cold sweat breaks out over my body. Mrs Truong must have told him. Oh God, she must have told him. "No!"

The doctor is forcing me out of the room. "Come on, they are upset, you need to wait outside."

"No, I need to be with Mai-Ling. I can't leave her, I have to help her."

"Not now."

"But . . ."

As the door closes behind me, I feel like I have been set adrift in an ocean of confusion. I cannot think straight. I should be there with Mai-Ling. She needs me, Mrs Truong needs me.

"Carrie Jones?"

I look up to see two police officers standing in the corridor.

"Carrie, we need to talk to you about an incident that occurred tonight."

"My best friend has just died in there, does anyone get that? I've already spoken to the police tonight so why are you harassing me again?" I can hardly get the words out through my grief. I cannot believe that this is the last time I will ever see Mai-Ling. I cannot let go of the hope that even now the doctors will somehow save her. It was just a stupid pill – everyone takes them. This is what happens to drug *addicts*, not people like us. But each time I think this the reality of the situation punches me in the guts and I feel like vomiting. "Leave me alone!"

"We have had a complaint from a Lun Pham who says you threw rocks at his car and then attacked him with a broken bottle."

"What? Is that why he's here? You *told* him I was here? No, I . . ."

As I stammer my answer, Pham steps into the corridor.

"I think Ms Jones and I may be able to sort this out if you give us a few minutes alone."

The policewoman is nodding. Everything is happening so fast. Pham is moving me to the end of the hallway, his cold bony hand digging into my arm. His breath stinks of stale tobacco as his face looms up against mine.

"You've killed her, you little slut. I know it and her mother knows it. The only people who don't are the police."

He has pinned me to the wall and is not letting up.

"You're not a child anymore Carrie. Even though you are only seventeen now, you will go to mainstream gaol the day you turn eighteen, and that's not far off, I'm guessing." He is smirking as he leans in close and whispers, "You know what happens to young girls in gaol, don't you?"

My mind is racing. I want to scream back at him but I am too scared the police will hear me. "It was an accident. I'm not a murderer. I'm not!"

"That's not how the law will see it. You gave her the drugs, it's the same as if you pulled out a gun and shot her."

"My father's a solicitor, he will fix it. He will make them see it was a mistake. You're just trying to scare me. I know all about you and if you say anything I will . . ." Fuck, what have I just done? Oh Jesus. His expression is so threatening it makes me cringe. I am trying to break free of his grip but he won't let go.

His words slash into my heart. "You say anything to anyone and I will spill your dirty little secret. Then, while you're in gaol, fighting off all the women who fancy you as their pretty little girlfriend, I will take your life apart piece by piece. One by one, the people you love will disappear and when you get out I'll come looking for you." He is laughing now like it's all a big joke, "You don't seriously think the police can touch me do you? I thought you were smarter than that Carrie."

I am struggling to escape but he is holding me tight. Tears are flowing down my face and I can't stop shaking. "Why are you doing this? If it wasn't for you Mai-Ling wouldn't be dead! What do you want from me?"

I can see the policewoman walking down the corridor towards us. As she nears us Pham leans closer, his breath hot on my ear. "You owe me Carrie, and you owe my family. Make no mistake: I'm going to make sure you pay your debt."

And now I finally get it. I've been out of my depth all along. In Mai-Ling's world, the rules have always been different. I'm in a game I can't ever possibly win. Only it isn't a game, is it? It's oh so real.

Oh fuck!

If you liked Ecstasy, you might like other titles in the Cutting Edge series.

The following is an extract from another Cutting Edge title. It's the first chapter of Gun Dog by Peter Lancett.

CHAPTER 1

It's all over the news again, in the papers and on television. Another kid has been shot dead, so it's all grieving parents telling us how little Billy was such a good boy and all. Telling us how little Billy only played football and was never involved in any trouble. Yeah, sure.

And of course the police are going to be moving heaven and earth, leaving no stone unturned. Yeah, right.

We've heard it all before. And there's the usual bunch of quotes from friends and neighbours. There they are, telling us what a nice neighbourhood it is and how shocking it all is and how they can't believe that it's happened right on their doorsteps. And of course, Princess Diana Syndrome has kicked in; you know, the bunches of flowers as close to the scene of the tragedy as the police will let them get. Mostly they're placed there by people who never even knew little Billy. It's on the telly, right, so everybody wants to be a part of it. What a bloody country this is.

And the reason I'm thinking about this now, while I'm riding home on my beaten-up BMX, is because I'm feeling the weight of what's in the canvas bag strapped to my back. It's books, mostly – as you'd expect, with me coming home from the library and all – but it's the other thing that's in there that puts the pressure on my mind. It's the gun.

Bad timing. It's bad timing that put the gun there. They say that timing is everything. I read that all the time. Well I got my timing all wrong, staying late at the library like that. Late, so that it's near dark when I turn onto the estate where I live. Late as I notice, as always, the line of young trees planted alongside the road that have been stripped or pulled out, the remains of some pathetic attempt by the council to make our area look nicer. Late as I notice, as always, the casual rubbish and the broken glass in the gutters. And inevitably, I notice the cans. Wherever you see the cans, you can pretty much picture the loose gangs of kids around my age and younger, even, wearing Burberry caps like it's standard issue uniform or something. You can hear them swearing, drinking, shouting, chucking stuff about. The kind of casual loutish behaviour that makes the rest of us feel uncomfortable... makes us cross over the road, walk quicker, head down, no eye contact. But, hey, I'm not judging them, I come from these streets just like they do. The estate is a mass of red brick semi-detached houses built in the fifties. A land fit for heroes is what my teacher says they were trying to build. Bet they never envisaged just how the children of heroes would turn out.

So anyway, like I say, I'm riding home from the library, and I'm deep into the estate. I see them, of course, as I approach

the boarded-up old pub, the Heart of Oak.
There are about seven or eight of them,
boys that I know from the estate and from
school. And I see the uniform of Burberry
and the hooded sweatshirts and trainers
and track-pants and they're fooling around
and spilling into the road. There's a lot
of shouting and swearing and raucous
humourless laughter. I hear a bottle smash.
And one of them is pissing up against the
wall of the pub. Right there in plain sight,
with the street-lamp like a stage spotlight
giving him a moment of fame. Chavs like
these are part of the local furniture here
where I live. They're not friends. And I'm
riding on the other side of the road and I'm
sure as hell not going to look over at them.
As often as not that's all it will take for them
to feel affronted and offended. And then it
would be time to be afraid. So I'm just going
to ride on by.

'Hey Davies, over here.'

I hear the words just as I see him step
out into the road and point at me. Roddy
Thompson is a big lad and boasts three

Anti-Social Behaviour Orders or ASBOs as they're commonly known. Dreamt up I reckon by some arrogant prat who lives in wealthy and isolated splendour with no idea how the rest of us actually live. Do they really think an ASBO, regarded as a badge of honour by the rest of the crew, could possibly be the answer? And just take a look at Roddy Thompson – do you think he fears one of those orders for one second? Yeah, right.

I bet you're wondering why I don't just pedal hard and get the hell away. Well if you're wondering that, then it's obvious you've never even *been* to an estate like mine, much less lived on one. And just where are you going to run to? So, swallowing back the pulse of fear-driven vomit that's leapt into my throat, I turn my bike towards big Roddy and coast to a halt right in front of where he's standing.

Big Roddy grips hold of the handlebars of my bike, but even he must know that I'm not going anywhere until he's finished with me. I see the letters that he's tattooed himself onto the fingers of his hand. I saw this old film once, and there was this ancient actor who had 'love' and 'hate' tattooed on his fingers, and I guess that must have been shocking, back then. Roddy has the letters K – U – C – F on the fingers that I'm looking at. I'll leave you to work out the actual word that he spelled. Probably the only word that he *can* spell.

'Where are you goin' Davies?'

'Just home.' I look beyond Roddy and the two or three others that have gathered around too close for my liking. In the dark shadows in an alcove in the far wall of the pub, I can see Sammy Williams. And someone else. A girl. Sammy has his back to me, but I know it's him. The girl I don't recognise, because she's beyond him and her back is pressed against the dark bricks. It's obvious to me, and to anyone else passing by, that they are having casual and brutal sex. Right there in the open. Like dogs.

Others of this little gang have surrounded me now. They're not saying anything but they stand very close, invading my space. It's uncomfortable, but I say nothing. I feel one of them tugging at the canvas bag strapped to my back. It's like he's pulling on it or leaning on it, so that I sag and have to brace myself against being pushed to the ground.

'What's in the bag?'

I turn my head, but can't work out which of the grinning louts has spoken.

'Just books.'

Even I can hear the little quiver of fear in my voice. I'd wanted to sound cool because they'll sense the slightest hint of fear like wild animals do. I've blown it.

'What do you want books for, you ponce? You think it *makes* you something?'

Snarled words from behind me again. A push at the bag on my back, so that I nearly fall over, bike and all. Roddy, gripping tight to the handlebars, holds it steady.

'No, no – I just...'

'You just think that school shit is going to get you somewhere.'

I'm looking at Roddy and he's looking past me to the kids behind as he speaks. I feel the pressure on my canvas bag loosen up. I'm standing straight. And I'm shaking, right? I'm scared now and no point hiding it. They could probably see *that* from space. I don't answer, just look past Roddy. I don't want to look anyone in the eye. Beyond Roddy I can see Sammy Williams starting to walk towards us. He has the dead eyes of a shark, but he doesn't move as smoothly. He's shuffling, stoop-shouldered and slack-jawed. Without a care in the world, he's wiping his dick on the *Nike* track pants he's wearing, then tucking it away. He doesn't care who's seen. Behind him, the girl is making a half-hearted effort to smooth down a short skirt. I don't recognise her, but then I'm not looking at her face. If she was ever wearing anything under that skirt before, she's making no effort to do so now. I've seen everything. And shc's seen me looking, but she doesn't care. I've seen enough of her to notice that she's nothing special.

Over-heavy make-up and hair pulled back tight in a 'Croydon face-lift'. Maybe she could be really pretty, but you couldn't really say with her looking as she does now. Sammy is right up behind Roddy and the girl is standing just behind Sammy and to one side. I feel like I'm on stage and that all eyes are upon me. I look up at Roddy and he must see that I am scared shitless, because he just grins and shakes his head.

'Nah, that school crap won't make you something. But this will.'

Roddy reaches inside his navy blue zip-up hooded sweatshirt... and I see three small patches sewn onto the arm as it flashes across, close to my face. ASBO ASBO ASBO – one for each of the three he's been given; a neat piss-take. But I'm not going to smile at it. It's all I can do not to whimper with fear. I'm expecting a knife – they all carry knives and they're all happy to use them. My eyes must be wide and wild and I can smell the cigarette smoke, the spliff smoke. I hear the rattle of a can in the gutter behind me.

And then there is Roddy's hand, right in front of my face. And it's not holding a knife at all. It's holding a gun. I must just gasp out loud because they're all laughing at me.

'This will make you something. This is what counts around here.'

He says this like we're standing in South Central Los Angeles or the Bronx in New York or something. But we're on a council estate in England. Since when did you have to have a gun to amount to something in a place like this?

I'm focused on the blue-black metal, shiny like there's a fine film of oil coating it. And the black rubber hand grip. Roddy points it right in my face.

'This could blow your head right off.'

He's not laughing as he says this. I'm not laughing either. Especially when he leans beyond me, and I feel my bag open and feel something being dropped inside. I know what that something is. Roddy has his hands on

my shoulders. He's looking me right in the eye, so that I have to look down.

'I want you to keep that for me for a while – don't mind, do you?' He sneers, all sarky. And I'm shaking my head even as I'm trembling. He seems happy with that reaction.

'That's good. Tell you what; you can have her if you want.' He turns his head and indicates the girl with the Croydon face-lift standing behind Sammy. I look up and see her taking a long drag from a cigarette and blowing the smoke out of her nostrils.

She notices me, but I look away because, to tell the truth, I'm embarrassed as much as I'm afraid.

'Go on, you can have her. We all have.'

I shake my head, I just want to go.

'Suit yourself. But look after that thing in your bag now. It will only be for a couple of days. Keep it safe.'

And then there's clear road in front of me and no hands holding my bike. So I pedal, but not fast, not like I'm running away. Even though I am. Behind me I hear something said and I don't quite catch the words. But then the girl's screeching voice is following me down the road and catching me, surrounding me.

'Ain't I good enough for you or summfin?'

She shouts a lot more but I'm not going to repeat those words.

So here I am, turning into my road, not far from my house. And like I say, the canvas bag on my back weighs heavier and heavier. I'm more alert than I've ever been and I notice the rubbish in the streets, the houses with well-tended gardens, and the ones where no one has cared. And, although it's a pleasant enough evening, I wonder that there are no people about on the streets or in those gardens. And I can't help thinking of Roddy holding that gun so close to my face. Roddy Thompson is fifteen years old. And a year behind me at school.

Life at the **CUTTING EDGE**
For more gritty reads in the same series

Scarred Lions
FANIE VILJOEN

A scarred, man-eating lion prowls the game reserve. Will Buyisiwe survive? And heal the wounds from the past?

Stained
JOANNE HICHENS

Crystal is a teenage mum in despair. Can't anyone see the tragedy unfolding? Her only hope is Grace next door.

The Finer Points of Becoming Machine
EMILY ANDREWS

Emma is a mess, like her suicide attempt, but everyone wants her to get better, don't they?

The Only Brother
CAIAS WARD

Sibling rivalry doesn't end at the grave – Andrew is still angry with his only brother, so angry he's hitting out at everyone, including his dad.

The Questions Within
TERESA SCHAEFFER

Scared to be gay?

Thrill Seekers
EDWINA SHAW

Douggie starts hearing voices, and there's nothing Brian can do as he watches his brother and his mates spiral out of control.

Ransom